Cowboy's Sweetheart

Sugar Coated Cowboys: Book #3

Stephanie Berget

Cowboy's Sweetheart
Copyright 2017: Stephanie Berget

Cover Design: RM Duffy

Other Titles by Stephanie Berget

Change of Heart Cowboys

Radio Rose

Salt Creek Cowboys

Sugarwater Ranch

Sugar Coated Cowboys

Gimme Some Sugar

Sweet Cowboy Kisses

Cowboy's Sweetheart

STEPHANIE BERGET

DEDICATION

To the Forepaugh Peak Barrel Racing Syndicate: Yo Curtis, Lee Trotter, Joan Harrington and Della Epler.

You pick me up, cheer me on, talk me down and urge me to buy just one more yard sale item. Thanks for being my friends and making my Arizona winters brighter.

STEPHANIE BERGET

CHAPTER ONE

Born at least a hundred years too late, Byron Garrett has finally found his place in the world. Even though he'll never own an acre of the Circle W, he couldn't imagine living anywhere else.

Although a thin rim of ice had nestled along the edge of the trough when he'd had caught his horse in the pre-dawn darkness, the chill of the early hours had warmed to one of the Northwest's spectacular autumn days. He'd shed his coat by noon and was now down to his T-shirt.

Turning toward the pine-covered mountain between him and the Circle W, he set off at a trot. After searching for years, Byron had finally found heaven on earth, away from the pressure of his father's attempts to remold him into the son he'd expected.

Byron's plan had been to work as a buckaroo for a few months then move on. Four years later, he'd changed his mind. He was here to stay.

Micah West, the owner of the ranch, had not only given him a job, the man had practically made him a part of the family. That thought brought a rare smile to Byron's face. He'd never felt a real part of a family before.

His Circle W family was as different from his biological

one as water and whiskey. As far as his mother and father were concerned, he was a showpiece to be trotted out when his father wanted to impress potential business partners. *Have you met my son, Byron? Full ride football scholarship at Penn State. We've had offers from several NFL teams. Yes, sir. Y'all are going to be watching him play football on Sundays.*

His mother intended to move to the top of the best social circles by having Byron marry into the right family. She'd ruthlessly worked toward this since he'd been a young teen.

Byron had ruined both their plans.

His sweet tempered little brother, who had the unfortunate luck to not be perfect in his parent's eyes, hadn't been introduced at all.

He shook the tension out of his shoulders. That shit was in his past now. He hadn't thought of his father for several months. And he wasn't going to waste another minute on the man.

Most of society thought a man had to be a little off in the head to be a hermit, but outside of his friendship with the West's, Byron was completely at ease with his solitary lifestyle. Out here, the only thing that cared what he did or didn't do was his horses, and as long as they got fed on time, they were content.

The pounding beat of Another One Bites The Dust pulsated through the mountain air. Byron smiled as he pulled his cell from his pocket. Queen was one of his favorite bands.

Tension constricted his shoulder muscles as he caught a glimpse of the caller ID. *Wilbur Garrett.* He turned the ringer off and slipped the phone back into his pocket. He was not going to let his father ruin a great day.

As he started through the pines toward the ranch house, the three-year-old gelding he was riding saw a ghost. There must have been a ghost, because there wasn't one threatening thing as far as Byron could see. The colt jumped and spun then blew air out its nostrils with a loud whoosh.

Rubbing his fingers through the horse's mane, Byron whispered. "Easy, Crater, easy."

Just as the colt started to relax, a jackrabbit jumped from a clump of sagebrush and raced for the cover of the pines. The young animal shook like a leaf in a windstorm.

Tracing a line between the gray and the white spots on Crater's neck with one finger, he scratched at a sweaty spot until the animal calmed enough to continue their ride back to the ranch. "Big, tough bunnies are the worst, aren't they, buddy?"

As he started up the trail, he felt a pulsation in his pocket. The phone was buzzing like a rattlesnake's tail. He'd turned the sound off, but forgot about the vibrate function. He grabbed it from his pocket and sure enough, it was his father—again.

Wilbur Garrett would go months without attempting to contact his son, but if he got a whiff of a NFL team looking to fill a hole in their offensive line, he was relentless.

Byron powered the phone down. "Crater, tomorrow we get a new number.

After closing the wire gate to the pasture, Byron took a moment to let his horse graze on some dry tufts of grass. The paint's coat was dark with sweat. This wasn't the easiest animal Byron had ever trained, but he had talent and fire and one day, he'd be a great one.

Byron rubbed his hand down Crater's neck. "Let's head home. Looks like for once, you're more tired than I am."

The colt was worn out from their all day ride, but Byron had ridden enough young ones to know tired didn't mean Crater couldn't fall apart with the right incentive. He gathered his reins, got hold of the saddle horn with one hand and mounted with a smooth move.

Crater stood like a rock.

Byron patted the colt's neck. "Good man."

The ranch house and barn stood in the distance, less than a half-mile away. A shower and one of Cary's home cooked meals would be an ideal end to a perfect day.

It didn't take long for the fast walking colt to reach the barnyard. As soon as they rounded the corner of the barn, the aroma of roasting meat made Byron's mouth water.

One of the perks of living on the Circle W, besides the fact that they pretty much left him alone, was Micah's wife's cooking. She was getting better at the meat and veggies part of the meal. Her pastries and pies had always been the best in the West.

As Byron shifted his weight to dismount, Crater's head came up, his ears pricked, and his body grew stiff with tension. Before Byron could settle back into the saddle, the colt whirled toward the house, snorted a loud whuff, and bogged his head.

Crater had missed his calling as rodeo bronc.

Byron tried to gather his reins, but blew a stirrup.

Ground is never soft when you're bucked off, but the barnyard dirt was packed like pavement from over one hundred years of use. Lucky he'd landed on his ass. He'd be sore but nothing was broken.

He watched as the paint colt continued his impression of a NFR saddle bronc. "You spavin-legged, mule headed, piece of shit!" he said under his breath.

Out of the corner of his eye, he saw movement. A colorful vision floated toward where he sat beside the round pen. Wisps of light, frothy material floated with the woman's movements. Long blonde curls bounced as she ran toward him.

Even the colt stopped bucking to watch her approach. He danced on his toes, ready to run at the slightest provocation.

Byron stood and held out his hand to stop the woman and returned his gaze to the colt.

"Are you okay?" she called, continuing to advance at a slower pace.

He whirled on her. He didn't want to yell. That might be all it would take for Crater to decide leaving was his best option. Luckily, his stare had its intended effect.

She froze in her tracks.

Byron turned back to the animal, crooning in a near whisper as he approached the scared colt. "Don't worry, little man. I won't let the big, bad lady near you." The paint was a bundle of nerves, but he stood until Byron could get a hand on the reins. "Let's get you put away."

He started toward the barn, but felt the change in the gelding the minute something behind them moved. Crater jumped and tried to push past him, slapping Byron in the jaw with his head. Byron took a minute to reassure the colt again, ignoring the pain, before turning to the woman. She'd stopped where she was, but the wind was whipping her skirt around her thighs.

High-heeled knee-high boots were as inappropriate for ranch wear as the rest of her costume. She looked like a woodland fairy or maybe one of those hippy girls he'd read about from the Seventies.

"Are you okay?" She stayed where she was, but didn't retreat. She hadn't taken his heavy-handed hint to leave. That's why he hung around horses, cats and dogs and not people. Hell, he even preferred hamsters.

If he'd been a friendlier man, he'd have taken a moment to explain why she was scaring the horse, and that he was fine. He could have asked her to leave him alone, but he'd found people rarely believed him if he politely told them he didn't want their company, so he'd quit.

Turning, he led the colt into the barn. He pulled his custom-made Wade saddle off the colt and stowed it in the tack room. He'd special ordered it from Hamley & Co. in Pendleton a few years earlier, and besides the horses he owned, it was one of his most prized possessions.

As he left the stall after turning the colt loose, Byron glanced out the door. The flower child stood where he'd left her, one hand raised, wiggling her fingers at him.

Just what he needed. A hippy do-gooder. She probably loved wolves and spotted owls. Thought they were people with fur and feathers.

It would only take a few minutes to throw a leaf of hay in Crater's manger and make his escape out the other end of the barn.

If he continued to walk away, even this flower child would take the hint that he didn't want her company. Right?

~-~

Vivi watched as the big man led his horse into the barn and began taking off his saddle. The animal was gorgeous, if dangerous. The sight of the man made her heart pound, but his attitude seemed the same as the horse— intimidating.

She'd always dreamed of owning a horse, but Mother would never have allowed it. You couldn't have a horse without dirt and dirt was one thing her mother controlled with an iron fist. Father took care of controlling everything else.

What her parents thought didn't matter anymore. She made her own decisions now. She was free as a bird, accountable to no one, although she wished with all her heart her twin brother, Sebastian, could be here to see this beautiful country and meet these cowboys.

When Sebastian had been killed by a distracted driver, she'd lost a piece of her heart. Now, she'd made up her mind to live enough for both of them.

Maybe the man hadn't heard her question about his injuries. She hated to think she'd done something to hurt him. Waiting until he had the horse in a pen, she entered the barn.

As she got near, he threw some hay into the feeder, glanced at her then strode away. Was this man rude or just reclusive? She'd found that people were often shy, and if she opened a conversation with them, she found a new friend.

If this cowboy was rude, she'd find out soon enough, but if he needed a friend . . . Well, then, she was good at that.

"Hey, cowboy. Are you okay?" she called out as she hurried after him.

He continued down the aisle toward the other end of the barn, apparently not hearing a word she said. He'd only spoken a couple of words to the horse, and they'd seemed garbled.

An idea popped into her head. Maybe the man was deaf. Even though her brother had been born deaf, he'd managed to speak a few words.

She ran until she was close enough to grab his shoulder. The muscles were hard beneath her fingers, and when he whirled to face her, she shrank back.

He was over six feet tall, way over.

She pulled in a calming breath and started signing. *My name is Vivi*. When he didn't respond, she continued. *I'm a guest at the Circle W. What's your name?*

The man's gaze shifted from her face to her hands and back. He raised his hands and spelled out B-Y-R-O-N one letter at a time.

She had been right. *Hello, Byron. I'm an artist. I'm delivering a life sized willow cow as a gift from Cary to Micah.* Her fingers flew.

He stood as if she were speaking Greek. Maybe he needed her to sign slower. *Would you like to see my work?* She watched as his brows drew down and his lips thinned.

"No. Thank you." His deep voice sent shivers down her spine, even though there wasn't much friendliness or interest in the three words.

"You aren't mute? Of course you aren't." She signed as she spoke. "My brother was born deaf, so I've signed all my life."

"Your brother?" His expression relaxed, and he

showed a moderate amount of interest for the first time since she'd started the conversation.

"My twin, actually. Sebastian." Her voice broke at the end of his name and she cleared her throat, forcing a smile. "So obviously, we weren't identical."

He raised his head and looked into her eyes for the first time. "Weren't?"

She didn't want to have this conversation. Sebastian's loss was still too new. It would always be too new. "You aren't deaf, are you?" His speech was clear and when the subject had turned to her brother she'd forgotten to sign.

"No. Why would you think that?" Byron stood, his broad, tanned hands on slender hips, the sleeves of his black T-shirt stretched by his biceps.

She couldn't help but notice the muscles cording his arms. Holy cow!

Her cheeks burned with embarrassment. She'd worked hard to have socially acceptable conversations with strangers, and she'd screwed this one up all the way. "When I talked to you outside, you didn't respond. I assumed. I'm sorry."

His gaze settled on her for a moment before he glanced toward the barn door. "Excuse me, ma'am. I have work to do." He turned on his heel and walked away.

Her lungs tightened, and she had trouble pulling in enough air. The tingling in her fingers spread an icy shadow up her arms. Cold hard power had radiated from Byron's face, spurring on the panic she'd fought hard to extinguish from her life.

Even though she felt like a chastised child, she walked from the barn to the house like she didn't have a care in the world. Working hard, she kept her pace slow and leisurely when all she wanted to do was run. Byron wasn't watching, she knew that, but just in case he was she let her hips sway with each step.

She opened the front door to the aroma of pot roast and the soft tones of Cary talking to her children in the kitchen. Vivi snuck upstairs and closed herself in her room.

Flopping onto the bed, she concentrated on breathing, visualizing her fantasy art studio. Thinking about her dreams helped calm the fear she'd fought hard to banish. The panic episodes had become fewer, but popped up every now and then. Mostly when she met overbearing people.

Pushing herself to her feet, she took a deep breath. She could sit in here and worry or she could get up and get going. After running a brush through her hair, she pushed it behind her ears. The blonde color suited her. Much better than the mousy brown she'd been born with. She focused a minute on the deep green of her eyes. God how she loved colored contacts. Those more than anything helped her feel like a changed woman. With the contacts in, she felt like she could hide who she'd been.

Sorting through her suitcase, she finished putting her clothes in the dresser. She'd been unpacking when she'd noticed a cowboy ride up the lane. He'd been mounted on the most beautiful horse she'd ever seen. It hadn't occurred to her that he'd be so private, so amazingly good-looking, and so powerful it made her heart pound.

Time to take her mind off the man in the barn, so she hurried down the stairs to a kitchen was filled with happy people, fresh bread and giggling kids.

Vivi ruffled Willa's wild red curls and picked Rodie up to whirl around the room. "How are my favorite munchkins?"

"You missed all the fun." Willa's elfin face spread into a grin. Several curly red tendrils escaped from her headband. "Mama dropped a whole bowl of bread dough and she said a bad word. Want to know what it was?"

Vivi watched Willa tease her mom and felt the bitter tang of remorse. She couldn't remember a time her mother had ever been playful. Her father wouldn't have tolerated the children's noisy banter.

The sound of Cary's voice brought her back to the present.

"Willa Wild West, when you're my age, you can say that word—maybe. Not before." When Willa only grinned, Cary pulled the girl into a one-armed hug.

"Tough day at the bakery?" Vivi leaned against the counter and handed the kids a cookie from the jar before taking one herself.

"You could say that. I'd have just thrown in the towel, but I promised Micah's guys fresh bread for dinner." She grabbed an apple from the sack on the counter and began peeling. "And a pie."

Nonchalance was never Vivi's greatest asset, but she gave it her best shot. "So I met one of your cowhands in the barn." She grabbed another cookie. Sugar was her best friend when her nerves gave her fits. Another thing Mother wouldn't approve of.

Cary gave her a quick look. "Which one?" She'd rolled out the crust and fitted it into the pan.

"Not sure of his name. Byron, maybe."

"Byron Garrett. He's been here for almost four years. When Clinton retired last summer, Micah offered him the job of foreman, but he's not much of a people person. He prefers to be alone. Nice guy though." Heaping the chopped apples into the crust, Cary sprinkled sugar and cinnamon on top. "A real sweetheart."

"Must not have been the same guy. Have you got two Byrons working here?"

"Nope, just the one. Why?" Cary finished making the pie and slipped it into the oven. Pouring two cups of coffee, she handed one to Vivi.

Vivi put her cup on the table and dropped into a chair, smoothing her multi-colored skirt across her knees. "Cause this one doesn't seem like a nice guy."

Cary burst out laughing. "Byron's not at his best with strangers. I should have warned you."

"Yes, you should have." Vivi unzipped her vest and

hung it on the back of the chair. This was her favorite outfit. The flowing material and colors remind her to live life and enjoy each day. "Does he ever lighten up? He looks like he chews on barbed wire for fun."

CHAPTER TWO

Byron kicked off his covers, stretched and rolled slowly to a sitting position. He hadn't had a good night's sleep in three days, and it wasn't the pain from being bucked off that was keeping him awake. Although he was plenty sore, he'd landed in the dirt many times through the years and survived.

No, every time he'd closed his eyes, thoughts of the hippy woman and her damned dress sashayed into his brain and took up residence.

During the day, he stayed away from the ranch house, choosing the steepest, rockiest fence lines to ride and the most unpredictable colts. The very real chance he'd get bucked off kept his mind on the job. But the vision of her curves encased in bright colors, her long silky hair blowing in the wind, crept into his mind just as he fell asleep, jarring him awake.

As a man who prided himself on his self-control, it pissed him off that he couldn't get her out of his brain. Peace of mind had been in short supply before he left Texas. Now, it was his most important objective, and he'd found it until Vivi waltzed into the barnyard.

A glance at his phone and he saw he'd better get

moving. He needed to get into the kitchen and grab something to eat before the rest of the house got up.

He'd learned long ago, if the back door was opened quickly it gave out a high-pitched squeal. Byron managed to squeeze through without a sound. He was reaching reached into the refrigerator to snag the roast beef when he heard someone say his name.

"Byron, you're up early." Cary stood behind him in a sweatshirt and jeans, her hair still mussed from sleep. "I have a favor to ask."

Byron didn't smile often, but this woman could bring out a good mood where no one else could. Even though they were about the same age, she was more of a mother to him than his own had ever been. At times, he was even a bit jealous of Willa and Rodie.

He knew, and he suspected Cary knew, he'd do anything she asked. He turned to face her.

Cary poured and handed him a cup of coffee then grabbed one for herself. Sitting in one of the high backed oak chairs, she motioned for him to take a seat. "You've found all the strays, right?"

"Got the last three yearlings a few days ago." The coffee was rich and smooth. He hadn't taken the time to get any the last few days. He'd missed it.

"My friend is staying with us for a while, and she'd love to learn to ride."

The warm feeling he'd been wrapped in turned to ice. Cary couldn't mean the hippy.

"You're so good with the horses, I think you'd be the best one to teach her."

"I've got more fence line to ride." He stood and poured the rest of the coffee into the sink and rinsed his cup. He could do without coffee. Without breakfast and lunch for that matter.

"Oh, I asked Micah, and he said that could wait a while. And it will only be for an hour or so in the afternoons. Come on." Cary topped off her cup then began pulling breakfast fixings out of the refrigerator. "You met Vivi the other day, didn't you?"

He'd met her, and he'd been a world-class jerk. A few hours a week helping her wouldn't hurt him, and it would give him a chance to apologize. "Send her out when she's ready." He turned and made his escape.

He could do this. The woman, Vivi, would grow tired of the horses the first time her ass and leg muscles burned from the effort. His brain latched on to the vision of her butt as she'd walked away that first day. You'd think he'd landed on his head the way he'd lost control of his thoughts.

Byron put one of Cary's saddles on a chestnut gelding then caught Crater. By the time he was tugging the paint's cinch snug, he heard shuffling footsteps behind him. He needed to apologize, but what would he say? Hi, I'm Byron, and I'm a natural born jackass.

When he didn't turn around, she cleared her throat. "Should I have called first to make an appointment?"

Byron could hear the amusement in her voice. Pretty, kind and a sense of humor. What the hell was he supposed to do with that?

He finished with the horse then turned. When he caught sight of her, he almost swallowed his tongue. The hippy was dressed in Wranglers that molded to her hips like a second skin. Her fuzzy pink sweater hugged her breasts, and Byron had to force his gaze to her face.

"Is this a bad time?" As she walked toward him, she shuffled her feet, her boot heels dragging in the dust. "Cary said you wanted to ride now, but I can come back."

"What's wrong with your feet?" He'd made up his mind to make the best of this for Cary's sake and was going for, if not an overly friendly vibe, at least not hostile. Seemed he hadn't gotten a handle on the not hostile yet. "You hurt?"

Her laugh rang out soft and sweet as a meadowlark's song. "I'm fine. Cary loaned me her boots for my lesson,

21

and they're a bit too big."

Her smile was a sight to see, and Byron found himself wondering how he could get her to laugh again. Disgusted with himself, he turned back to the horse. "Go wait at the arena. I'll bring your horse out."

"Can I help you with anything?"

He didn't answer—couldn't answer. Just shook his head. The sight of her in that pretty pink sweater had his tongue tied up like a calf at a rodeo. He knew exactly why Cary wanted him to teach the hippy to ride. She was a matchmaker of the highest order.

It was obvious to him that this woman came from money. She would leave the Circle W as soon as she got tired of pretending to be a cowgirl. She wasn't ranch people. If she did stay around, she'd want him to change.

Hell, his dad had made it perfectly clear that with this lifestyle, he wasn't good enough.

Better to keep his distance and wait for her to go.

He led Crater and the sorrel to the arena then waved the hippy inside. "Get on."

Instead of doing what he'd ordered, she moved to the horse's head and began stroking its face. "You are a pretty one. Yes you are. What's your name, big guy? Huh, what's your name?"

"He can't answer. You know that, right?" Byron talked to his animals all the time. Why was it so irritating when she did the same thing? "He's just a horse."

Vivi turned to face him, her eyebrows pushed down and her full lush lips thinned by aggravation. She kept stroking the horse, but the tone of her voice changed. "You seem so angry with me. Have I done something to you? Is it because I scared your horse that first day? If so, I am sorry."

She had him there. She hadn't done a thing except keep him up at night. He damned sure wasn't going to tell her that embarrassing piece of information. "I've got a job to do, and we're wasting time." There, that ought to be enough of an explanation.

"Really? Cary told me this was part of your job, but if you're too busy, I'll go back in the house." She made a shooing motion with her hands. "Go on. Do your important man stuff."

She took another minute to run her fingers through the sorrel's mane and stroke his neck, before shuffling toward the arena gate.

The boots must be several sizes too big, and he caught himself smiling. He lifted the reins over the horse's head. "Come on back." He should apologize, again, but he couldn't count the times he'd apologized to his parents, and it had never gotten him anywhere.

She stopped then slowly turned, being careful to keep her feet balanced in the boots. After staring at him for a moment, she grinned. "If you really want me to."

~-~

So far, the cowboy had been demanding and closed minded. Maybe that was a big man thing. Father had been almost Byron's size, but she had to admit, Byron didn't seem to have the mean streak or the need to control that dominated her father's disposition.

Vivi'd promised herself she wouldn't be intimidated ever again and now was as good a time as any for her to step up. "Thanks, I appreciate your taking the time. What do I do now?"

"Have you ever ridden a horse before?" Byron checked the cinch then turned to her.

"Are you kidding? My parents wouldn't let us near an animal. They carry germs, you know." Her laugh died, and she had to work to keep the regret from showing.

"Everything has germs." Byron lowered the stirrup then rested his hand on the horse's neck.

"Mother was a bit paranoid. Father didn't like animals. They didn't always do what he said." Regret, relief and resolve pulsed through her. The past was staying in the past. She pulled in a deep breath and plastered the grin on her face again. "I love animals though."

For the first time, the big man looked at her and seemed to see her, not some insect to swat away. He stepped back a foot or so and motioned her to come closer to the horse. Placing his hands on her shoulders, he positioned her beside the saddle. "Put your left foot in the stirrup, and I'll help you on."

She did as he asked. When his strong hands settled on her waist and lifted her into the saddle, she almost gasped out loud. The warmth of his hands disappeared as soon as she was settled. She looked down on him. "This is a tall horse."

"Not really." He made some adjustments to the stirrups so they fit her short legs. "Hold the reins like this and bump him with your feet."

"Bump?"

With a shake of his head, he took her ankle and tapped it softly against the horse's ribs. At his touch, another tingle ran over her nerves.

"Okay." She adjusted her reins in her hand, trying to mimic the way he'd shown her. Then she looked down on him. "I need to know something before we go any farther."

When he just stared at her, she continued. "What's his name?" She couldn't possibly ask this beautiful animal to carry her around on his back and not know his name, but she knew without being told that Byron would think she was foolish if she voiced her thoughts.

"Worry." Byron stepped away. "Now bump him with your feet."

"Worry, why Worry? That seems like an odd name for such a pretty horse." The copper color of his coat gleamed in the sun. The light blonde of his mane and tail were close to the color she'd chosen for her own hair.

"Worry is short for No Worries. He's the horse we put

all the dudes on when they come to visit Cary and Micah." Apparently tiring of her questions, he took hold of the reins and led her around the pen.

"This is amazing. Lucky you. You get to do this every day." The old Viola would never have had the opportunity to ride a horse. She couldn't contain the smile that spread across her face. Cross another item off Vivi's bucket list. "What a great job."

Byron glanced over his shoulder. "The best." His glare was gone, and she saw the barest start of a smile before he turned away.

"Can I try by myself?" Her heartbeat sped up at the thought of controlling this huge animal. Riding a horse had been a lifelong dream.

Byron left her and walked to the center of the arena.

Vivi bit her lip and looked things over. She had to keep her feet in the stirrups to keep the boots from falling off. She wiggled the toes of the boots, but instead of moving, Worry dropped his head and relaxed. When she looked at Byron he had a smile on his face. It disappeared as soon as he caught her watching.

Laughing at her was he? She lifted both legs and kicked hard. Worry's head came up, and he started off across the pen at the most uncomfortable gait. The beast was trying to buck her off just like the other horse had done to Byron.

Vivi tipped to one side, dropped the reins and hung on to the saddle horn with both hands. She pulled her knees up, clinging to the saddle like a tick. Her left boot dropped to the ground.

Byron was at her side before she fell, steadying her with hands on her thigh and waist.

She reached up and pushed her hair out of her face. Her cheeks burned with embarrassment and anger. "This animal is a bucking bronco. You did that on purpose."

His expression sobered. "I wouldn't do that to you." He pulled his hands away, bent and picked up her boot. "I

25

said bump, you kicked. Worry thought you were asking him to trot."

She thought a minute, running what had happened through her mind. "Can you show me how to stay on when he does that?"

He almost chuckled. "Why don't we learn to walk first?" His hand was just as warm when it clasped her calf as it had been on her waist. He slid the boot on her foot and put it in the stirrup.

This time when she asked, Worry walked away with a slow, gentle gait. She felt a rush of power when she turned the animal back toward Byron. They worked for most of an hour before Byron called the lesson to a halt. "This is enough for today. You're going to be sore as it is."

As she swung her leg over Worry's back, Byron helped her down. She turned and stood in the circle of his arms. Holy neutrons! The heat coming from his gaze nearly set her heart on fire, and she leaned toward him.

He jerked away like she had Spotted Fever.

To cover her embarrassment, she went on the offensive. "I'm a pretty good rider already, right? Maybe even a prodigy."

He only grunted, but his elusive smile played at the corners of his mouth.

"One of these days, I might even win the Grand Prix like National Velvet. I'll give you all the credit as my trainer."

"National Velvet rode in the Grand National. The Grand Prix is a dressage competition. I don't do either of those."

"Don't you ever look on the bright side, or the funny side or the happy side of anything?" Vivi poked him in the shoulder, trying to get him to lighten up.

"Look lady. I'm only supposed to be a riding instructor, not your life coach. We're done here." He tried to take Worry's reins out of her hands, but she held on.

This lightening-him-up thing hadn't work out like she'd

planned. His sour attitude reminded her of Father. When he let go of the reins, she schooled her features into a nondescript expression. "Would you mind if I helped you put Worry away?"

With a wave of his hand indicating that she should follow, he headed for the barn.

They worked in near silence. Byron's words were clipped as he told her how to put the halter on Worry. She didn't ask the questions bouncing around in her brain.

By the time they had the horse back in his pen, the tension in Byron's shoulders seemed to have eased.

"Thank you for helping me today. That's the most fun I've had since I went skydiving in New Mexico." She giggled as his eyes rounded.

His stoic expression morphed into horror. "You jumped out of a plane?"

"Yes, and I went rock climbing in Arizona. You've got to take chances in life. If not, you miss all the fun." She'd started with a smile on her face, but as she spoke, she thought of Sebastian. The skydiving, rock climbing and horseback riding had been partly for him, too.

"The highest I want to get off the ground is the back of a horse. Don't need any help dying by doing insane things." Byron settled the saddle blanket on the rack in the tack room and hung up the bridle. "That's just nuts."

"No, that's living my life." She wasn't nuts, crazy or insane. "I don't want to die without living first." She paused. My parents were frightened of anything they couldn't control and did their best to make me frightened too."

He looked at her for a moment, and she didn't think she'd imagined his barely perceptible nod before walking away.

STEPHANIE BERGET

CHAPTER THREE

Cary dropped the last handful of potatoes and carrots on top of the second pork roast and slid the pan in the oven. It took a lot of food to fill up the ranch hands at the Circle W. A pastry chef by trade, she'd had to learn ranch cooking when she'd arrived at the Circle W a few years ago.

She'd been running from her past and had run right into her future.

"Mom, Rodie is touching me again."

As Willa came to stand beside her, an innocent look on her face, Cary reached out automatically and redid the girl's ponytail. The eleven year old's red curls seemed to escape at will. "And what did you do to him?"

"I was minding my own business, just like you and Pa said, drawing pictures." Willa widened her eyes and tried unsuccessfully for innocence, but Cary knew her stepdaughter well.

"And?" Cary leaned against the counter and waited.

"Well." Willa drew out the word for emphasis. "I drew me and my horse running barrels. My brown pencil broke, so I had to borrow Rodie's crayons. I had to."

"Was Rodie using the crayons?"

"He's a little boy. He doesn't need all the colors." She flopped down in a chair. "I do."

"So he was using them." Cary schooled her features into a frown even though she wanted to laugh out loud at her daughter's antics. "And you took them?"

"I borrowed them."

Willa's demeanor melted as she realized she wasn't going to win this one. "I'll go give them back." She stood and started toward the living room, dragging her feet.

"Willa?" Cary waited as Willa turned to face her. "I think it would be nice if you'd color with your brother for a while, too. He loves it when you do things with him."

Willa thought for a moment then nodded. "Okay, I can help him learn to color in the lines." With a smile, she hurried out of the room.

Willa Wild West. Willa's birth mother had thought the name appropriate, but Cary didn't agree. The girl was as sweet as she was outgoing.

Cary grabbed a big mixing bowl and began making a double batch of Waldorf Salad. The men seemed to love the gooey mixture as much as the children.

Footsteps rang across the floor and she looked up to see Vivi entering the kitchen.

"I need a beer," Vivi said as she sank into a chair. "Make that a shot of Fireball."

"It's not even noon yet. How about a cup of coffee instead." Cary filled a mug and handed it to Vivi. "First lesson hard?"

She took a sip of the hot liquid and sighed. "I love the horse. Worry is beautiful and kind. It's the cowboy I don't understand. He hates me, and I don't know what I did to deserve that."

"Byron's shy." Cary grabbed a Coke from the fridge and popped the top.

"You said that already. Shy I get, but grumpy? A couple of times he started to relax then I'd say something and boom—he'd be Oscar the Grouch again. Could he be embarrassed because I saw him get bucked off that horse the first day?"

"Do you want me to talk to him? Or Micah?" Cary hadn't known Vivi long, but the woman had been relentlessly positive about all things. It was unsettling to see her upset.

"Oh, heck no!" Vivi ran her fingers through her hair, pushing it behind her ears. She raised her voice to a high singsong. "Byron, daddy and mommy say you have to be nice to me. That would go over great, wouldn't it?"

The sound of the kids squabbling filtered into the kitchen.

"Do you need to referee that?" Vivi attempted a smile.

"No, they'll figure it out themselves." Cary took a long swallow of the soda. She gave the pudding, pineapple and marshmallow mixture another stir then covered the massive bowl with plastic wrap and stowed it in the refrigerator. "Give Byron some time."

"I guess you're right. Maybe I'm overreacting." Vivi stood and grinned, trying to look like the pretty, positive person Cary had met a year ago. "I'm off to call the shipping company and see when Micah's birthday present will be here."

"He's going to be so surprised."

"Who's going to be surprised? You promised no surprise party for me." Micah's deep voice sent a shiver down Cary's spine. Even in her fondest dreams, she'd never thought she'd end up here with a man who loved her and the best two kids anywhere. "Everything isn't about you, Micah. We were just talking about Byron." She hoped the change of subject was smooth enough Micah wouldn't question her later.

"What about him? Or do I want to know?" Micah picked up her Coke and drank the rest. "I'm pretty sure I don't."

Vivi folded her arms across her chest. "It's nothing."

"He's not being very friendly to Vivi," Cary said,

ignoring the frown Vivi threw her way.

Micah filled a glass with water from the pitcher in the refrigerator, drank half and turned to the women. "Being nice isn't in his job description. Gathering cows and breaking colts is, and he's one of the best."

"Cary's overreacting." Vivi smiled at Micah, frowned at Cary and disappeared into the other room before either of them could say more.

~-~

Leaning back against a bale of straw, Byron smiled as a black and white kitten climbed his shirt, pausing with each tiny step to pull its claws from the fabric. Two more were scampering over his legs, backs arched, doing their best impressions of tiny killing machines.

Old Myrtle, one of the ranch cats, had disappeared five days ago and Byron found the three little puff balls crying in the haystack. He and Cary had mixed up some glop that the kittens devoured, and he spent a few minutes every morning just enjoying the kitten's antics.

He hadn't seen the woman, Vivi, for the last two days. She'd probably decided riding wasn't for her. With her pretty clothes and put together look, she almost reminded him of his mother. Except, Vivi smiled all the time, at everyone. His mother only smiled if a person was worth her time, and then it never reached her eyes.

He stood and dusted off his hands. As he stepped out of the straw bale pen he'd made for the kitties, the black and white kitten latched onto his pants leg. "You can't come with me, Cruiser. The cows would take one look at you and stomp you into the mud." He gently disentangled the kitten and placed it back into the pen.

"What did you name the other two?"

Vivi's soft voice sent a jolt of pleasure through his body, and he quickly squashed the sensation. "They're barn cats. Don't need names."

"But didn't you just call that one Cruiser?" She bent and scooped up the kitten and held it to her face.

"Yeah." No use denying what she already knew.

"Why Cruiser?" Vivi put the first kitten back and picked up the gray tabby.

"Like a black and white police cruiser, I guess." He watched her stroke the tiny head and watched the kitten relax in her arms. "I've got to go."

"What's this one's name?" She pointed to the calico backed into the corner watching them warily. "And that one?"

Byron looked at the two kittens. He hadn't gotten around to naming them yet. He was trying not to name them at all. They needed to become ranch cats not pets, but he loved animals. "Cat, I guess."

Her smile was bright, and she showered all that warmth on him. "That won't do at all. They'll be confused when you call them." She climbed over the straw bale, placed the gray on the floor and reached for the calico.

The runt hissed and swiped its tiny paw at her hand, drawing a bit of blood. Vivi didn't miss a beat. She sank to the ground. "Hey, tiny friend. I'm not going to hurt you." Her soft melodic voice was as hypnotizing to Byron as it was to the kitten.

Vivi inched her hand forward and touched the baby on the head. Within a few minutes, the kitten was in her lap. Not completely relaxed, but allowing Vivi to pet it.

"I'm not sure about a name for the little gray one, but this one is Eleanor."

"Eleanor? What kind of name is that for a cat?" Byron shook his head as he straddled the straw bale and sat down. He couldn't wait to hear her reasoning for that name.

"This kitten is feisty, knows her own mind and isn't afraid to take on anyone. Just like Eleanor Roosevelt." She shifted her gaze from the kitten to Byron. "It is a girl, isn't it?"

"You're in luck because Eleanor would be a terrible name for a tomcat."

The smile that spread across her face was a sight to behold, and he caught himself smiling back at her. She gave him a light punch to the thigh. "You made a joke, big guy."

Big guy. That was the title his father used to introduce him to important people. *Come on over here and meet the big guy. My son, the big guy. There's not a running back in the country that can get past the big guy here.*

There were times Byron wasn't sure that his father remembered his name. It was like his whole worth as a human being was tied to his size. His worth as a son sure was.

Byron stood and walked out of the room and began saddling the first of the colts he had lined up to ride today. As he snugged the cinch, he felt a soft touch on his arm.

"I'm sorry. I wasn't making fun of you. It's just that I hadn't heard you joke around before, and that was funny." Vivi stepped back as he turned.

He relaxed his jaw and tried to slow his breathing. This wasn't Vivi's fault. She'd made an innocent comment, and he'd overreacted. God, he'd thought he was over this. He couldn't manage a smile yet, but he tried not to frown at her. "Not your fault." He owed her more of an explanation, but he didn't have it in him. Not right now. Maybe never. "I've got horses to ride."

She nibbled on her lip. "Can I ride with you? I'll try to keep my stupid questions to a minimum, and you can ignore the ones that escape."

Byron could see the excitement shining in her eyes as she tried to control her eagerness to ride again. Why the hell couldn't she be interested in something Cary could teach her? He didn't have a good excuse to say no, so he shrugged.

"Catch Worry and brush him like I showed you the other day. I'll help you saddle him." He walked out of the barn to turn the young horse into the arena. Leaning on the fence, he watched as the animal jumped and bucked and generally enjoyed life. How long had it been since Byron had enjoyed anything besides gathering cows and riding colts? Not since his early football days.

And if he didn't stop these maudlin thoughts he'd be mired in bitter memories. He made his way back into the barn to find her with her arms wrapped around Worry's neck, her face buried in his mane. As he got closer, he could hear her talking.

"What are we going to do about that guy, Worry? He's so sad."

So she felt sorry for him, did she? Byron stormed into the tack room and grabbed Worry's saddle and blanket. He smoothed the blanket on the chestnut's back and threw up the saddle before turning to her. "You and Worry don't need to worry about me. I'm doing just fine."

He heard a snicker then a snort.

"I know the whole world revolves about you Byron, but Worry and I were talking about Willa's old dog, Chase." She pointed to the corner, and there sat Willa's graying border collie.

"Willa said he'd too crippled up to work anymore, and he's sad. Worry and I thought we might let him go with us when I get to be a good enough rider to leave the arena." She was in full out laughter by this time. "Too bad you're in such fine shape, or you could join us."

He knew Vivi would do about anything to keep from embarrassing another person, but today, she seemed to take a great deal of satisfaction in the burning color of his cheeks.

CHAPTER FOUR

And to her utter shock, he ended up smiling. A small smile, but a smile none-the-less. And he'd told another joke.

She wanted to let out her newly acquired snark, but the last time she'd said something, he'd gotten angry and quit talking to her.

What could she say that wouldn't set him off? Just smile and be polite? She shook her head. When her father had died, the one promise she'd made to herself what that she wasn't changing to make anyone else happy.

"Another joke. That's two in a row." She stood her ground waiting for him to stomp off. When he didn't, she relaxed the slightest bit. "Is that a personal best?"

He didn't answer her, but he didn't leave either. Instead, he finished saddling Worry and handed her the reins. "Let's go, Annie Oakley."

"Be still my beating heart. The man has a sense of humor." She hurried after him, and she was almost sure she heard a chuckle.

Vivi managed to climb aboard Worry without any help from Byron. *Dumb move there, Vivi.* She'd liked the feel of his strong hands as he'd helped her on the before.

He caught the colt, bridled him then stepped on.

Vivi had this riding thing down as long as Worry didn't get out of a walk. She'd managed to turn him both ways and stop and back him under Byron's watchful eye. She was feeling like she'd nailed it until Byron told her to trot.

Who the hell ever thought of this as a means of transportation? She clung to the saddle horn with one hand and pulled back on the reins with the other. "I know you're not too fond of me, but if you kill me right here in the arena, it'll be a little obvious, don't you think?" Worry stopped, and Vivi leaned over the saddle horn trying to catch her breath.

"I like you." Byron's brow was furrowed.

"So, not speaking, and ignoring a person is how you show affection? I pity your girlfriend." Vivi's breathing slowed to normal, and she prepared to try the trotting thing again. When Byron didn't answer, she looked up.

"I don't ignore you." He looked truly confused as if it had never occurred to him that not speaking was bad manners.

"Look, Cary told me you're shy."

"I'm not shy. I just don't like to be around people, is all." Byron settled deeper into his saddle and walked the colt in a circle around Vivi and Worry. "Everyone wants to change who I am and what I want to be."

"Maybe they just want you to be polite." Vivi twisted her head, trying to keep Byron in view. This was the closest thing to a normal conversation she'd ever had with him. Despite everything, she enjoyed his company, and she knew all about people not accepting who you were. "Oh, and I like you, too."

Byron stopped the horse, asked him to back a step or two then loosened his reins. The animal reached over and snuffled Worry's mane. "Why?"

She'd been watching the colt and Worry but looked up at the question. "Why what?"

A hint of blush colored Byron's cheeks and he ducked

his head. "Never mind. Try trotting again and stand up in your stirrups."

Why did she like him? Was that what he was asking. Whatever he'd been about to say, he'd decided against repeating. She gathered her reins and held them like Byron had showed her and clucked to Worry. The horse shook his head and walked. Vivi bumped his sides with her feet and clucked again. Worry broke into a slow trot. She bounced from side to side until she heard Byron. "Stand up."

By the end of the lesson, she'd almost mastered posting at the trot. "Not bad for a city girl." Byron held Worry while she dismounted then led both horses to the barn.

"Let me try unsaddling him." Vivi watched until Byron nodded, then flipped the stirrup over the saddle seat like she'd seen Byron do during her earlier riding lessons. She worked the latigo loose and pulled the saddle and blanket from Worry's back. When Byron had thrown it on, the saddle looked like it didn't weigh much, but she staggered under the weight. "Wow, this is a full body workout just taking care of these guys."

Byron took the saddle from her but left the blanket. "It'll put hair on your chest for sure."

"You are just full of jokes and witty sayings today, aren't you?"

Byron handed her a soft brush and indicated Worry. He began to brush down the horse he'd ridden. "My friend's grandpa used to say that to us all the time."

She brushed away the sweat. "Where are you from?"

He didn't answer, and when she turned to look, he was concentrating on working a tangle out of the colt's mane.

"That's okay. None of my business." She hurried on, wanting to keep him talking. "I'm from Massachusetts. Born and raised in Cambridge. Father was the head of the chemical engineering department at MIT. Mother was a physics professor at Harvard before she retired to raise my brother and me."

He was watching her, not saying anything, but not walking away so she continued. "I like it back there, but I'm having so much fun traveling around the country. America has so many beautiful places. Have you ever been to Zion National Park? I've never seen anything like it."

She glanced up to see if he was still listening.

Byron shook his head. "Nope. I like it here just fine. Don't need to travel to be happy." He put both horses away and turned to Vivi. "Lunch should be ready."

She expected him to turn and walk away, but he waited for her to join him. "I'm starved."

Byron kept his distance from her, moving a few feet to her right, as if she might give him a spontaneous hug or something equally awful. He was talking though, and that was better than the other times she'd spent with him.

As they entered the kitchen, Cary looked up, and her eyebrows rose in surprise. "You two have a good time riding?"

Byron sat in front of a huge pile of sandwiches and grabbed the top one. Cary set a glass of milk in front of him and pushed a mixing bowl filled with chips to the center of the table. "She did good," he said after chewing and swallowing some of the sandwich. "Worry took care of her."

"He speaks," Vivi said as she sat down beside him. She glanced at Cary, a wide smile lighting her face. "Byron's teaching me to ride, and I'm teaching Byron basic social skills. I think it might even be working."

~-~

The hippy woman never let up. She kept digging at him. With anyone else, he'd have walked away, but there was something about her, something besides her looks. She was pretty, but more than that, she hadn't let him intimidate her. He could get rid of most people by glowering, the tougher ones by towering over them, using his size. Neither tactic had worked on Vivi.

There were a couple of times she seemed to back away then caught herself and stood her ground. And almost always with a smile. It was tough to push someone away who wouldn't leave.

He didn't want her around all the time, he didn't want anyone around all the time, but he had to admit, she was better than most.

"Yeah," he said under his breath as he kept his gaze on the sandwich. "She's going to have me dancing the Virginia Reel for the cotillion and drinking tea from bitty china cups with my pinky finger stuck out like a flag."

Cary stood and walked over to Byron, placing her palm against his forehead.

He jerked back. "What the hell?"

"Just checking your temperature. You've been here four years, and I've never heard you say that many words at one time. I'm not sure you've said that many words the whole time you've been here."

He stood, shaking his head. "Women. Can't leave a man alone." He grabbed a fist full of sandwiches and the glass of milk and hurried out the back door.

Just before the door latch clicked shut, he swore he could hear a snort and a muffled giggle.

What had gotten into him? He never talked unless he had to, and he kept those occasions to a minimum. Somehow, and it pained him to admit this, trading barbs with Vivi had become kind of fun.

Byron detoured around the side of the barn and opened old Chase's kennel. Settling on a straw bale, he tore off a piece of sandwich and tossed it to the dog then took a bite himself. After they'd finished off lunch, Chase curled up at his feet.

"So the hippy woman has been letting you out, huh?" The dog's tail thumped a couple of times, and he looked up at Byron, the gray around his face a little more pronounced each month. "What are we going to do with her?"

It took a moment for the question to register. Seemed he'd lost control of his mind. He wasn't going to do anything with her. He was going back to his quiet life. He was going to hand over responsibility for the woman to Chase. That way everyone would be happy.

"She's all yours, buddy." The dog glanced at Byron. The look said it all. *You may fool yourself with that, but you haven't fooled me.*

Byron snorted and Chase managed one more wag of his tail. "Come on then. I've got a colt to work in the round pen. You can help me with this one."

Byron set the empty glass on the bale, and made his way around the barn to the horse pens with Chase limping at his heels.

He'd worked the colt about twenty minutes when he saw Vivi approaching. This ranch was too small for the two of them. He concentrated on the horse and continued as if he hadn't seen her.

"Why are you doing that?" Her voice was loud enough that he couldn't pretend he hadn't heard. "Why do you have his head tied to the side with the rein?"

Legitimate question. "He learns to give to pressure. If he turns his head, the rein loosens. It helps for when I get on him."

"How long do you leave it like that?" She stood on something, making her tall enough to see over the sides of the pen.

"Not too long. Don't want it to be a punishment. This is the best way to teach them to give."

"Cool! I didn't know you could do that." There was that grin again. "But I don't know anything about horses."

"You know how to get on, make them walk and trot and turn and back up. That's more than most people." He turned his attention back to the colt, but found himself waiting for her response.

"Thanks."

"Thanks for what. It's the truth." He clucked and encouraged the colt to trot around the pen. This colt was small for his age, but this line of breeding was known for that. By the time the animal was seven, he'd be a big solid horse. For now, Byron was giving him extra time to grow.

Vivi wasn't talking. She hadn't been quiet this long since he'd first met her. When he looked up, she turned away. He thought he saw her make a quick swipe at her eyes.

"You okay?"

She looked over her shoulder, bestowing that smile on him again, although it was a little rocky this time. "I'm great. Who wouldn't be living here?"

"Got something in your eye then?" He stopped the colt and tied his head to the other side. He left the animal standing there to get used to the pressure and walked to Vivi.

"Yeah, that must be it." She'd recovered from whatever had been bothering her and gave him a light punch in the shoulder. "Must be allergies."

Byron watched as sorrow then determination raced across her expressive face and decided to change the subject. "You said you were from Massachusetts?" When she nodded, he continued. "What did you do there?"

Her brows drew down, and a frown settled on her face. "Do? What do you mean?" She stepped down off the bucket she'd been standing on and leaned against the fence, her arms crossed.

"You know. You said your mom home schooled you, but you must have had some hobbies, something you enjoyed doing for fun." He grabbed another bucket, turned it upside down and sat down. "Do you ski?"

Vivi dropped onto her own bucket. A sigh escaped her, and she looked at the sky. "I studied. I guess you'd say science was my hobby."

Science? Byron hadn't minded science in school. He'd even been in an accelerated class and had pulled all As, but he'd never in any world consider it a hobby. He studied Vivi's face and noticed an undercurrent of sadness before she saw him watching and schooled her features. "Science?"

"Yeah. Specifically physics. My mother and father were big on schooling."

"That's not big, that's obsessed."

She burst out laughing at that. "You're right. Father was the obsessed one. Mother went along with whatever he said." Her laughter stopped as fast as it had started. She dropped her chin into her hands and closed her eyes. "Commanded would be a more accurate word."

"Did you say you have a brother?" The silence drug out until Byron became uncomfortable.

Vivi stood and gave him a look filled with despair. "Had." Without another word, she disappeared behind the barn.

His happy-go-lucky, free spirited hippy girl was hiding some unhappy secrets.

CHAPTER FIVE

Lester Charters studied the numbers on the computer screen in front of him and nodded in satisfaction. With Charters Asset Management Company calling the shots, Viola Beckett's accounts were performing well. They were beating the market by several percentage points.

Charters and Charlie Monroe, Viola's maternal grandfather, met in grade school, and the two men had remained lifelong friends until the day Charlie died fifteen years ago. After years of tinkering on countless inventions, Charlie hit the jackpot when he made a miniature sound recognition device.

Hear Me Now could be attached to almost any item. By tuning it to the sound of your voice, losing things became a thing of the past. Call out to your glasses or keys, and a recorded voice said, "I'm here." An affordable price made it a must have for nearly every person on the planet.

When the money began rolling in, Charlie hired Lester and his money management firm to set up a trust for his daughter and each of his grandchildren. All the money belonged to Viola now, not that she'd had much use for it.

At the sound of a knock on his office door, he closed the laptop.

"Mr. Charters? I have Ms. Beckett on the phone." As soon as he nodded, the secretary stepped out and closed the door.

Lester took a moment to collect his thoughts before picking up the phone. "Viola, dear, how are you?" He opened the laptop again and settled back into his office chair.

"Hi, Mr. Charters. I'm good. Is something wrong?"

Lester had always felt a little sorry for Viola and her brother, Sebastian. Their father had been so overbearing it was hard for anyone, including Charlie, to be around him for long.

Charlie's daughter was the only one who seemed to like the man, but Charlie hadn't trusted him. Even though his daughter had been married to Beckett for over twenty years, Charlie had set the trusts up so Beckett couldn't get his hands on the money.

After the accident, the millions became Viola's.

"No, no, no, nothing's wrong." He waited a minute for effect. "The market hasn't been performing as well as we'd like. I wanted to check with you once again and see if you'd like me to explain what we're doing with your money."

He heard Viola sigh.

"I trust you, Mr. Charters. Grandy trusted you to handle his money, and you've always taken care of me."

"If you're sure, Viola. I'm doing my best for you. Do you have a new address? We're getting ready to send out your statement. You'll notice a small increase in our fees. Not what we'd planned, but we're working on some new investments, and I'm sure I'll have better news next quarter."

To his complete delight, Viola didn't want anything to do with the day to day handling of her money.

"Just send any correspondence to the PO box you have on file. I've seen some beautiful places in my travels, but I haven't found home yet."

They said their good-byes and Lester hung up. He'd known Viola since she and her brother were born. She'd been a quiet, studious little girl and had grown into an introverted young woman. Even though Viola was getting out, seeing the world now, he'd often wondered if she'd be happier if she didn't have any money at all.

~-~

Vivi fitted her toothbrush into the holder and washed out the sink. When she found her home, she was going to paint her bath in the soft sage green of Cary's guest room walls. The conversation with Mr. Charters the day before was the same as always.

Maybe he was right. Maybe she should make an effort to learn more about her assets. If, for some reason, Mr. Charters couldn't handle her money anymore, she should have some knowledge of her investments. When she found a home, that is one of the first things she'd learn.

She brushed her hair with more force than was necessary. If it weren't for her art, she'd have given all the money to charity right after her father died. The money was Grandy's. He'd earned it, not her.

She'd seen the damage the desire for riches had done to her father. She'd have given it to him, but her grandfather made sure Father couldn't get his hands on a penny.

The tension between the two men had colored every holiday and family get-together until Grandy died, filled with suspicion and hostility, and she and Sebastian had learned to tread lightly.

She worked several various colored ribbons into the single braid down her back. Pulling on royal purple leggings, she topped the outfit off with a thigh length black and white animal print T-shirt and a wide sparkly belt. Her purple, pink and lime green scarf hung to her waist.

The bright colors helped with the depression she felt whenever she spent too much time thinking of her past.

47

She shook her head, shaking off the bad feelings. Life was too short to spend worrying about things she couldn't change.

Vivi found Cary in the kitchen putting the last of the breakfast dishes in the dishwasher. "So are we still on for a trip to town?" Cary asked as she wiped down the counter. "I need to pick up a few things at Foodtown, and I thought we'd stop in for coffee and something to eat at the café."

Vivi felt her mood lift on exposure to her friend's sunny disposition. "I'm ready."

"I want to introduce you to Pansy. You two are going to be friends the minute you meet."

"Where is Rodie?" On a usual morning the four year old was in the kitchen, chattering at anyone who would listen. He was one smart little boy and never forgot a thing he heard. She'd noticed the ranch hands were careful of their language when Rodie was around. All the employees seemed respectful of the women and children. Maybe that was Micah's doing.

"He's with his dad today. They're going to the cow sale in Burns. Rodie took some of his savings in case one goes cheap enough." Cary hung the dishtowel on the hanger and grabbed a jacket from the hook by the kitchen door. "Micah isn't worried, but I know my son. He'll find something to buy one of these days and with only forty-seven dollars and eleven cents, I'm not sure we'll want it on the place."

Vivi laughed. She hoped Rodie found something to buy. She had no doubt, Micah would make sure the animal was healthy, and as for looks, Rodie would love a runt of a calf just as much as a registered one.

With Willa in school and Rodie with his dad, today would be a girl's day out. Only three hundred residents called East Hope, Oregon home, but the town had everything necessary for day to day living.

Cary parked the pickup in front of a long, low building

with Foodtown in big letters along the edge of the roof.

They hadn't made it two feet inside the store when a woman came hurrying from the back and wrapped Cary in a big hug. "'Bout time you girls made it to town." She turned to Vivi. "You must be Vivi Beckett. I'm Millie. I own this place."

Millie's hair was a disconcerting candy apple red, but Vivi decided right there she'd try the color on her own hair one day. She held out her hand and smiled. "Nice to meet you, Millie. This is your store?"

"I've owned this place for over thirty years. When my husband died, I thought about selling out, but then what would I do with my time?" Millie turned to the girl at the cash register. "Take care of things, Lilly. I'll be in the back."

"Careful here," Millie said over her shoulder as she pointed at a large crack in the faded linoleum.

They followed Millie down a jam-packed aisle. Walmart this wasn't, but Vivi loved the small town vibe.

They walked through the narrow aisles and entered a large room behind the meat counter. Millie wrestled a brown corrugated box down from a stack, pulled a box cutter out of her pocket and slit the tape sealing the top. After digging through a pile of things on an old scarred desk, she found a small white paper bag. She pulled on a thin plastic glove and grabbed a handful of something from the box.

"I buy these for Micah, but you can help yourself if you like them."

Vivi found her hand filled with chocolate covered raisins. She raised an eyebrow at Cary.

"These are Micah's favorites. Millie takes good care of him."

"Well, I agree with Micah. These are one of my favorites. I first found them in a little general store in Mississippi." Vivi popped one in her mouth. The sweetness of the chocolate mixed with the raisins. "My mother wasn't big on sweets. Said they weren't good for us."

Millie's eyes widened then a smile spread across her face. "Have I got a treat for you." Millie pulled down three more boxes, opened them and put a handful of each in a small white bag and handed it to Vivi. "There's chocolate covered cinnamon bears, orange slices and malted milk balls. No one should live their life without these babies."

Vivi dug through and tried one of each kind. "These are all good, but the orange slices are my favorite."

Millie filled one of the bags nearly to the top and handed it to Cary. "This ought to keep Micah happy for a while."

"I'm sure it will." Cary turned to Vivi. "Try the orange slices and the malted milk balls at the same time. This is gourmet candy at its best." She and Millie looked at each other and laughed.

"What's so funny?" Vivi popped another candy into her mouth, letting the chocolate melt on her tongue as she rolled the top of the bag closed. She'd missed many things in her very strict childhood. It was difficult to not gorge on things many people took for granted.

Millie wiped her eyes. "Gourmet candy. I buy this stuff in bulk as you can see. Not one redeeming value except the taste. I started buying the raisins because I heard Micah loved them, and the rest of the town requested other flavors."

Cary rummaged through her purse and handed Millie a list. "I only need a few things today. If you don't mind, I'm going to introduce Vivi to Pansy. Can I pick this up later?"

Millie ran her finger down the short list. "We've got all of this. Come on back by whenever you get done, and I'll have it packed up. And tell Pansy I got her special order."

The length of East Hope's Main Street was less than three blocks long. Situated diagonally across the intersection of Main and First streets from Foodtown sat the Five and Diner, the town's only café and main meeting place.

The first time Vivi had been in a small-town café was when she'd left Massachusetts for her trip cross country after father had died. As with every small town, Vivi had fallen in love. The warm atmosphere and good food made her feel at home.

A bell jangled as Cary opened the glass door to the café and heads turned to watch as they crossed the room and took seats at the counter.

"I love these." Vivi touched the cool metal of the Wall-o-matic Jukebox song selector with reverence. "The first one I ever saw was in Virginia." She dug a coin out of her purse, flipped through the pages and selected a song. Johnny Cash's deep voice filled the room as he sang about walking the line.

Cary pointed to several large color photos lining the wall above the kitchen pass through. I Love Lucy, Marilyn Monroe and Cleopatra were in full color and costume. "That's our Pansy."

"The lady that runs this place? Really?" Before Vivi could ask more, a brunette with a braid down to her waist came through the swinging door from the kitchen. Her face lit up at the sight of Cary, and she hurried down the aisle.

"Why didn't you tell me you were coming into town? I'd have fixed something special." The brunette turned to Vivi and held out her hand. "I'm Pansy."

Vivi looked from Pansy to Cary to the pictures on the wall and back to Pansy.

"It's the proverbial long story, but—well, the costumes served their purpose at the time." Pansy placed a plastic menu in front of the women and pulled a pad out of her apron pocket. "What can I get you?"

Cary looked at Vivi. "Coffee and one of your fantastic sticky buns."

"For lunch?" Vivi drew her attention back from the

photos.

Cary patted Vivi's shoulder like she was a toddler. "Taste Pansy's Supremely Sticky buns first then tell me they aren't appropriate for any meal."

Vivi thought a moment then nodded. "I'm in, and will you make one to go?"

Cary looked at Vivi. "You'll have more than enough to take some home for later. One roll usually lasts me three meals."

Vivi felt the heat rise in her cheeks. "I thought I'd take one home to Byron."

"Byron has a big sweet tooth. Take him one of these and you'll have a friend for life."

CHAPTER SIX

Byron knew trouble when he saw it—or heard it. Ever since Cary had mentioned the Harvest Dance, he'd made himself scarce. It was just an innocent remark, made at dinner one night, but Byron noticed the look in her eye.

He'd watched a few years ago when Cary had played matchmaker to Pansy and Kade. Despite his doubts, the Cary-orchestrated romance had turned out okay, but Pansy and Kade had a history. Byron didn't want or need a history with anyone.

He paused by the gate and zipped up his jacket. The weather had turned from warm late fall to chilly early winter in the space of a couple of days. He rode the four-wheeler through the pasture, checking cattle. While he worked, his thoughts wandered back to what he was sure was Cary's plan.

He almost felt sorry for her.

Byron didn't dance. He'd never liked the crowds or trying to make small talk with the girls he'd been forced to ask out by either his mother or well-meaning friends. The only time he'd enjoyed himself was when he'd taken his brother as his date.

Watching Milty wave his arms as he swayed to the

music always made him smile. Milty enjoyed everything. A few different people had dared to laugh at his brother. One look from Byron, and they'd not only quit snickering, they'd joined in the dance.

After setting out salt blocks and making sure the pairs they'd gathered were where they were supposed to be, he headed for home, once again, missing Chase's company. The barn came into view. He'd have to be careful to stay out of sight until the others left for the dance.

He parked the four-wheeler below the hill and snuck up to the back door of the barn. With everyone else getting ready, he figured he'd be safe spending a few minutes feeding the kittens.

He'd scooped kibble into the bowl set high on the ledge in the tack room. A few weeks ago, he'd made a ramp so the cats could get up but the dogs couldn't. At the sound of the scoop, the three kittens came running. The little calico had gotten over her initial fear and now was his buddy.

She crawled up his leg then climbed his shirt and settled on his shoulder. "Hey, Camo. How's my mouse killing machine?"

As he stroked the kitten's soft fur, he heard footsteps in the barn aisle. And him without an escape route.

Cary stuck her head in the door. "Aww, they are so cute." She scooped up the gray kitten he'd named Stormy and cuddled him to her chest. "I saved you some dinner."

"Thanks, Cary, but I'm going to eat in town tonight." He hadn't been going to do that, but there was no way was he hanging around.

"Oh, you're going to the dance." The kitten began furiously wiggling, and Cary bent to sit the little thing on the ground.

Byron heaved a sigh. If he handled this right, maybe he'd convince Cary to leave him alone. "No."

She stopped and tilted her head as if she was thinking. "You can come with Micah and I. Vivi will feel less like a third wheel with someone else there."

"Aw, Cary. I—"

"Please, Byron. You don't have to stay all night. Just for an hour or so. Please."

And what the hell was he supposed to do with that. Cary had gathered him up and become a friend when he'd needed one. She didn't ask favors very often. She usually respected his boundaries, especially when he'd made the boundaries very plain. "I don't like to dance."

"I know. You don't have to. Just talk to Vivi for a while and maybe introduce her to a few friends."

"You know I don't have any friends." Byron thought that might get through to the woman.

Her face brightened. "Wonderful. Then she'll give you someone to talk to at the dance, too. Thanks, Byron. You're the best." And she was gone. Just like that. Before he could convince her this wasn't the best idea.

The conversation run through his head again as he tried to figure out where he'd lost the battle. With a sigh, he stood.

He could do an hour.

If he took his truck, he could stay just long enough to be polite then let Vivi ride home with Micah and Cary. It wouldn't hurt him to spend an hour talking to the townspeople, and he hadn't seen Pansy all summer. With his hours at the ranch and Pansy's at the café, they didn't have much time to socialize.

He'd been wrong before. About not having friends. He and Pansy had become friends when she'd come to town three years ago, mainly because they were both a little different, and they didn't have expectations about being anything more.

Byron had been dubious when Kade had first come back into Pansy's life, but Kade seemed to really love her. Good thing, too. He could beat the shit out of that little bronc rider.

He headed for the bungalow.

The clock said almost eight. He threaded his horsehair belt through the loops on his pressed Wranglers then pulled on his best boots. Why he was going to all this trouble, he didn't know. Digging his good hat out of the box he kept it in, he settled the black felt on his head just as someone knocked on the door.

The vision that stood on the doorstep—Vivi in a full length, body-hugging purple dress and heels—took his breath away. He'd been expecting jeans and boots. There was something to be said for being a city girl.

Her hair hung in loose curls to below her shoulders and for the first time since he'd met her, she had jewelry, lots of jewelry. An antique squash blossom necklace circled her slender neck and every bracelet that had ever been made lined her wrists. At least it looked that way to Byron. Engraved silver earrings graced her ears, and three large silver and turquoise rings were on her fingers. When she moved, everything tinkled.

"Ready to go?" She gave a shimmy and did a twirl. "I don't know how to do these western dances, well, any dances, but I can't wait for you to teach me."

Byron didn't dance. He should have stopped her right there, and told her to find another teacher but his tongue was pasted to the roof of his mouth. His brain had stalled, and he was having a hard time keeping his eyes from bugging out of his head.

Grabbing his coat from the hook by the door, he spent the seconds it took to shrug his arms into the sleeves attempting to do something he normally did on auto-pilot. Think!

When they'd gotten to the pickup, Byron opened the passenger door.

Vivi studied the interior, glanced at him then tried to hike her skirt high enough to modestly climb in. Without running boards, there was no way.

"Could you turn your back, please?" She twirled her finger and gave him an embarrassed grin.

"Turn my back?"

She pointed at her skirt. "The only way I can climb in is if I pull this up to my waist." She faced the truck and started working her skirt up her legs.

Although Byron would have liked to watch the show, he put his hands on her shoulders and turned her to face him. "Let me help." Wrapping his hands around her waist, he lifted her onto the seat.

Their faces were even, her lips just inches away. He hesitated and before he could decide whether to give in to his desire to kiss her, she leaned in and kissed him. "Thanks."

The touch was soft and light, more of a feathering across his lips, but he wanted more, with a craving that shocked him. He leaned into her, breathing in the sweet scent that was Vivi, and brushed his lips across hers. If he kept this up, they'd never make it to the dance. With dogged determination, he dropped his arms, stepped away and closed the truck door.

The feel of her lips had his mind doing cartwheels, and he forced himself to concentrate on turning the key, putting the truck into gear and driving toward East Hope.

While he kept quiet, Vivi chattered non-stop, giving him nervous glances from time to time. On the north edge of town, a warm yellow light glowed from the Grange Hall windows, and the parking lot was filled to overflowing. The nearest spot was in front of Foodtown several blocks away.

He parked and turned toward Vivi.

She had her knit shawl wrapped tight around her shoulders. Shivers shook her body.

"I'm an idiot." She pointed one pink tipped finger at her this dress. "The weather was so warm today I didn't realize it would cool off so quickly. It'll be warmer inside, won't it?"

Byron jumped out of the truck, hurried around to the passenger door. He slipped out of his jacket and settled it around Vivi's shoulders.

"Won't you be cold?" She tried to slide it off and hand it back, but he tugged it back into place and buttoned the top button.

"I'm used to this." He helped her down, keeping his hands at her waist a moment longer than needed. He could smell her citrus scent and feel her warmth. For the second time tonight, if he didn't move his mind on to other things—like the way she'd change if they became serious—they might not make it to the dance at all.

Byron stepped back, but she reached out and threaded her fingers through his, then led him toward the dance.

~-~

Golden light, country music and laughter poured through the open doors of the East Hope Grange Hall. The sound of voices was barely discernable over the guitars and drums.

"I've never been to a dance, let alone one where the whole town joined in. I couldn't wait. Byron held back, but in her excitement, she pulled him toward the faded clapboard building.

When she stopped short in the doorway, Byron bumped into her, but she didn't move or apologize. She leaned back into his strength, and he stifled the desire to wrap his arms around her waist.

"That looks hard." She glanced at Byron over her shoulder. "The dancing. Can you do that?"

"I can. I don't."

"Ah, you choose not to. I understand that." Then she took his hand and pulled him onto the dance floor.

At that moment, the music changed from a Texas Two-step to *She's Everything* by Brad Paisley. Paisley had never been Byron's number one choice for artist of the year, but with Vivi swaying to the music, the song just became his new favorite.

Smiling, she moved closer and wrapped her arms around his neck. As she swayed to the beat of the music, he froze. She tipped back her head enough to see his eyes. "You just stand here, and I'll try to figure this out myself." Then she laid her head against his chest.

He'd warned her he didn't dance. If he stood like a statue, maybe she'd get the hint and go find someone else to bother, but the thought of Vivi dancing with one of the other men made his lungs clench. He didn't like to dance, and that was a fact, but standing in the corner watching Vivi in someone else's arms was not going to happen.

He wrapped his arms around her waist and let the music carry him away. The song ended too soon, and he held her waiting for the music to start up again.

Damn local band. When Dusty Reynolds, the lead singer of Call Me Country, called for a break, Byron could have strangled him.

Vivi took a step back, taking all her sweet scented warmth with her. "Want to get something to drink?"

As if he had any choice. "Sure. Lemonade or tea?"

She ducked her head and looked at him from beneath her lashes. "Anything is fine with me."

As they crossed the floor to where the local Baptist ladies had set up a table with soft drinks and cookies, Carl, one of Micah's other employees, stopped him. "We got a bottle of Fireball outside. Want some?"

Vivi turned her attention to Carl and smiled. "What's Fireball?"

Carl stammered before he got control of his tongue.

Byron knew the feeling well.

"Well, well, it's cinnamon whiskey, ma'am." Carl turned to Byron. "Sorry, I didn't realize you were with Miss Vivi."

Carl looked at Byron and took a step back. "Not right now, Carl."

Vivi put her hand on Byron's chest. "I've never tried that. Could we?"

He had the reputation of being the toughest man on

the Circle W, even though he'd never once resorted to violence. All anyone ever had to do was put this woman in front of him, and he became a total wuss.

"Are you sure you don't want lemonade?"

"I've had lemonade and tea. I'd love to try the Fireball." She took his hand and ran her thumb over the back. "Unless you don't want to. I can try it another time."

Carl moved closer to Vivi and pointed toward the door. "Come on with me for a moment. We'll find Byron when we come back."

Byron didn't drink much. He'd learned years ago he was uncomfortable being out of control, but no way was he letting Vivi go outside by herself. He put his arm around her shoulder and followed Carl out the door. Just off to the side stood a group of men and women, all of whom he knew.

"Hey, By-ron." The man dragged out his name into several beats. Ronnie Snap was an ass. He'd tried to ride bucking horses at the small local rodeos. Byron had never seen him make eight, but Ronnie played up the rodeo cowboy part. "You didn't make it to practice last Thursday—again. You really have become a hermit."

Byron ignored him and led Vivi to the other side of the group.

As usual, Ronnie couldn't take a hint. "And who is this? She's much too pretty to hang around with a ranch hand."

Vivi looked at Byron, confusion written across her face.

Micah stood from where he'd leaned against the battered Chevy truck. "Ranch hand?"

Ronnie looked at Micah and laughed. "You're the owner so you don't count, but everyone knows the only guys who work on ranches are the ones who can't make it riding bucking horses." No one had ever accused Ronnie of being smart.

When Micah went to step forward, Byron waved him away. He tightened his grip on Vivi's hand and turned to go back inside the building. He could crush this idiot with both hands tied behind his back, but it wasn't worth it. His size had nothing to do with the person he'd become.

As they reached the door, Vivi wiggled her hand loose and turned back to Ronnie. "I thought I recognized you."

Ronnie's chest puffed out like an overfilled balloon. "You saw me ride?"

Vivi's smile would have melted chocolate, and she tapped her cheek with her finger. "No, I haven't been to a rodeo yet. You're the guy who took Cary's groceries to the truck the other day. You work for Millie, right?"

The crowd erupted in laughter, and Byron leaned against the wall of the grange hall to watch the show.

"What is it that Millie calls you?" Vivi smiled at Ronnie like they were best friends. Giggles from the others got louder the longer Ronnie didn't answer.

"Dumb ass," Millie said as she made her way through the parked cars toward the group. "It's my pet name for him."

Ronnie's face flushed red. Without another word, he hurried through the parked cars, away from the crowd.

Vivi brought a cup of amber liquid over to where Byron stood. He liked watching her move. She should have been a dancer. Maybe she was. He'd never asked.

"This is a great beverage. So warming." She took another sip then held out the cup to him.

"You know what else is?" Then he uttered a word he thought he'd never say to a woman. "Dancing."

CHAPTER SEVEN

Vivi opened her eyes to the bright reds and blues of a Pendleton blanket hanging on the wall. Rough wood shiplap paneling rose to meet log beams. The flickering of flames from the wood stove danced shadows across the walls and gave the room an otherworldly feel.

She rolled to her back, waited a second for the room to stop spinning then took in her surroundings. A handmade wedding ring quilt on the twin bed she was snuggled into was done in shades of brown and tan with a splash of turquoise here and there.

Hefted herself onto her elbows, she made sure not to aggravate the pounding in her head. This was Byron's house, but Byron wasn't here. She dropped back down, trying to bring the evening before into focus.

The one dance she'd had with Byron had been magical. She'd met several new friends and one jerk, enjoyed the cinnamon whiskey. After that things got a bit blurry. She had a vague memory of Cary asking if she was all right. The memory of Byron carrying her to the truck must have been a dream.

What the hell was in that stuff anyway?

Things were coming back now. She didn't remember

the drive home, but remembered Byron lifting her out of the truck. The air had been icy, and she'd welcomed the warmth of his arms around her. "The house is locked, and I'm not sure when Micah and Cary will be home."

"I can sleep in the truck. I'm not that cold." She was, but she'd have been fine if Byron had wrapped her in his coat.

"Close your eyes. I've got a better idea."

The chill of the night air had brushed against her skin as she snuggled deeper into Byron's arms. A girl could get used to this. "You're pretty strong, you know."

Byron had tightened his grip as he mounted the steps to his cabin. The door clicked shut, closing out the wind, and the heat from the pot-bellied stove licked at her skin.

He'd put her in his bed, leaning down to brush her hair off her face, and that was her last memory until this morning.

Faint streaks of light outlined the hills to the east. Vivi untangled her long skirt from around her legs and sat up, taking an extra moment to give her brain time to stop spinning.

A small kitchen was nestled in one corner. A door to what must be the bathroom was on the other wall. Washing her face and rinsing her mouth out did wonders for how she felt.

Just as she finished pulling Byron's comb through her tangled hair, the door opened and a gust of cold air accompanied him into the house.

What was she supposed to say to a man she'd spent the night with? Sure, nothing happened, she was sure of that, but she'd never been in this situation before. "So how long did we stay at the dance?"

Byron's smile spread across his face. "I gotta give it to you. You're a party animal. We didn't get back to the ranch until... let's see, it must have been ten o'clock at least."

Her head snapped up. "Ten? That's all? And we didn't get to dance again." She dropped into the recliner next to the woodstove and buried her head in her hands. "I made a fool of myself, didn't I?"

"Nah." Byron stuffed a couple more pieces of wood into the stove then went to the kitchen and dug a heavy cast iron pan from beneath the stove. "How do eggs sound?"

"I got drunk?" She couldn't keep the question from her voice.

"You were fine until the second glass of Fireball. You don't drink much, do you?" Byron lit the burner then pulled eggs, bacon and hash browns from the refrigerator.

She had made a fool of herself. "I don't drink at all."

Byron looked at her with a straight face, but she could see the smile in his eyes. "No kidding?"

"Sebastian and I were allowed to have a glass of wine with dinner once in a while. Father didn't believe in using stimulants. I've tried several kinds of alcohol during my travels, but I never really liked the taste. I guess I didn't handle it very well." How would she face these people who'd taken her in and been so nice? "The first time I'm invited to a social function and I get drunk."

Byron broke six eggs into a bowl and mixed them with a fork. He laid the bacon slices in one pan, and Vivi could hear the crack and sizzle as they hit the hot metal. "You weren't drunk, you were tipsy. I thought it was time to come home, but when we got here, the house was locked." After pouring the scrambled eggs into the other pan, he stirred them with a plastic spatula. "Hungry?"

They didn't speak much as they ate, but when they'd finished, Vivi cleaned the table, and Byron poured them each another cup of coffee.

"Seems like you parents were against lots of things." He sat down, took a sip and looked her in the eye. "Were they religious?"

How to explain her family. Through the years, she'd found it better to keep quiet about them or to change the subject. She'd begun to deflect when the truth came out instead.

"Father was strict." She stopped and pulled in a deep breath. "That's an understatement."

Byron studied his coffee and waited.

"He was always right. He knew it, and my mother knew it. There was no room in his family for mistakes." She worked to drive off the memories that crept back in whenever she let down her guard. "We all learned early to do things his way."

When she stopped speaking, Byron spoke, his voice quiet. "Did he hit you?"

Vivi jumped, startled and stared at him. "Oh, no. He wasn't like that." How did she explain that Father hadn't needed to use violence? The mental control had been enough.

"So, what then?" Byron took her hand. "A person can be abusive without hitting."

As much as she wanted to confide in someone—not Byron—and not today. She'd spent the last year working to convince herself she wasn't crazy. She needed someone to tell her she'd done, was doing, the right thing, but she was too embarrassed to tell this man. His father was beyond controlling, but Byron had found the strength to leave. He hadn't let a narcissist ruin his life.

"You don't have to tell me, but if you want to talk about it, I might understand, and I promise I won't judge." He stood and refilled the cups.

She took a sip of the hot coffee, swallowed wrong and had a coughing fit. When she'd regained control, she looked him in the eye. "He never hit us. Just looking at him standing there, the I'm-in-control-here look on his face, was enough to make us toe the line."

"Sounds like an asshole." The grumbly sound of his voice caused her to giggle.

"He was an asshole. One of the best. He's gone now, and I don't feel bad about that at all. It does bother me that Sebastian never got out from under his control." Her voice broke on the last few words and she stood, trying to smooth some of the wrinkles out of her dress. Like that made any difference.

Byron took her chin in his hand and lifted until she met his gaze. "This isn't your fault."

"I know, but I was the stronger twin. I should have protected him."

"So you were supposed to protect your whole family from a man that had made it his life's work to control you? Sounds like a lot for one person." He wrapped his arms around her, and she worked hard to keep her tears in check. No one had ever seen her life that way before.

~-~

The rumble of a truck's engine coming down the drive caught their attention. A delivery van with the logo of the shipping company Vivi had hired to send Micah's sculpture was parked near the front porch. The driver stood talking to Cary.

Excitement and unease sparred with each other, making her stomach jump. Would Micah and Cary like her art or think it was a bunch of sticks? She turned to Byron, faking calm as best she could. "I can't believe the shipping company sent the crate to East Hope, British Columbia instead of East Hope, Oregon. I was beginning to wonder if it would ever arrive."

As if reading her mind, Byron smiled. "They're going to love it."

"How do you know? You haven't seen it."

"I've seen pictures, and I know you."

Vivi looked at her dress, wrinkles making it obvious she'd slept in it. "I can't go out like this. What will Cary think?"

"No one here cares if your dress is wrinkled or where you slept." Byron pulled her across the driveway. "But go change if you need to, and I'll see if the driver needs help."

Vivi followed Byron to the truck. He was right. She

didn't owe an explanation to anyone.

"This is perfect timing," Cary said as they approached. "Micah went to town for grain. We can get this set up before he gets back."

"Can I help?" Willa's high voice caught Byron's attention. Her boots clattered against the worn wooden steps as she raced out of the house.

Byron took her hand. "Come on. You can be the boss."

He watched as Vivi's shoulders stiffened with tension. She chewed on her lip, and her fingers clenched together. "Are you okay?"

"I will be if Cary likes this." She gave him a shaky grin as she followed the driver to the back of the truck.

"Let's get it unloaded and find out." In a few long strides, Byron was seated in the forklift and removed a huge crate from the truck. Cary asked him to position it on the grassy spot in the center of the circular drive.

Cary looked at Vivi. "You do the honors."

Byron grabbed a crowbar from the forklift and eased the wooden top from the crate. He pried the sides apart, revealing a stunning life-sized longhorn steer, made out of willow sticks.

While Willa danced around the sculpture with oohs and ahhs, Byron circled Vivi's handiwork. She'd told him she made things from sticks, but he hadn't expected this.

Vivi ran her hands over the sculpture until she was satisfied no damage had been done during the shipping. Her gaze when she faced Cary was filled with worry.

"This is so cool," Willa said, her voice high with excitement. "This is cooler than when Taylor Barker's mom made a whole set of dishes from wood."

That brought Cary to life. "Vivi, I knew it was going to be great, but the pictures didn't do it justice. This is amazing. You're amazing." Cary gave Vivi a hug. "I can't wait for Micah to get home now. This is going to blow him away."

It for sure blew Byron away. Who knew you could make statues from sticks? "You really made this?"

"Yeah. This is what I do."

Byron walked around the beast, knelt and looked underneath then studied the head. The proportions were exact, the workmanship precise. "I can't believe it."

"I can!" Willa said. "But how are we going to keep Rodie off of it. He already wants to be a bull rider." She reached up and stroked the fine twigs that made up the steer's nose. "It's so real it makes me want to find it some hay."

Vivi's musical laugh caught his attention. Pride had replaced her apprehension. "That's the best thing about my animals. You don't have to feed them."

They heard the engine of Micah's truck just before it turned into the drive. Cary picked up the nearest side of the box and held it up to hide the present. "I can't wait to see his face."

Micah climbed out of the truck then grabbed Rodie around the waist and carried him to the group. "What's this?"

Rodie wiggled until his father put him down then ran to look behind the piece of wood Cary was holding up. "Pa, it's a cow."

Cary dragged the piece back so Micah could see. "Happy Birthday, honey."

"My birthday was a month ago." Micah came closer, and Byron noticed Vivi chewing on a fingernail.

"I know, but I didn't order it in time for Vivi to get done. Better late than never." Cary took her husband's arm. "Do you like it?"

Byron could see the same question reflected in Vivi's eyes, deep green pools swimming with unease.

"This is really something," Micah said, still looking at the steer.

"But do you like it?" The small quaver in Vivi's voice gave away her apprehension.

Micah turned to Vivi. "I've never seen anything like this. It's good."

Vivi reached out and laid her hand on the statue's rump. She stared for a moment then raised her gaze to Cary's.

Cary put her arm through her husband's. "Micah's a man of few words but that means he likes it."

Vivi almost melted with relief, and Byron couldn't stop himself from reaching out and taking her hand.

She leaned against him, her voice barely discernable. "My father would have hated it."

~-~

Lester Charters opened the email from Viola Beckett with some trepidation. In the years since her father had died, he'd only gotten one email from the young woman. And that was to tell him where to send her mail while she traveled across the country.

He'd had total control during the dark time when she'd cared for her incapacitated her father. She'd never cared much about the money. When Beckett died, she'd escaped from the family home and told him to do what he'd thought best with the fortune.

That was just the way he liked it.

He clicked on the email.

Dear Mr. Charters,

I just wanted to give you a heads up on an idea I have been playing with for a while. I want to open an art studio somewhere out west. I'm going to look around for a suitable site. Sisters, Oregon looks nice, as well as Sun Valley, Idaho and Leavenworth, Washington. They're all tourist towns and might be a good location. Nothing is set in stone yet, but I didn't want to catch you by surprise.

All the best,

Viola Beckett

He did a quick search of Sisters, Oregon and property prices. Then he looked at Sun Valley and Leavenworth. This crazy idea of hers wouldn't do at all.

He took his time before writing her back.

Dear Viola,

It is so nice to hear from you. I'm glad you're having a good time with your hobby, and it's nice to see you making plans to move on with your life. With the market like it is, now would not be the optimal time to pull money out of your mutual funds. My advice is to keep looking, but plan on waiting another year or so.

There's no use rushing into things after all.

I'll contact you as soon as I feel it's the best time to move funds from the market to real estate.

Take care,

Lester Charters

He hit send and sat back feeling better. Viola had never refused to take his advice before and he was sure she'd do as he advised now. All he needed was a few more months to repay some investors. Money he'd needed to keep him solvent and money she'd never miss.

CHAPTER EIGHT

Byron looked up from saddling the colt to marvel at Vivi's steer. He was still in awe. How did someone look at sticks and envision an animal, or anything other than a stick?

He had one of the sorrel colts saddled and in the round pen when Vivi called out to him across the yard. "I'm feeling very confident on Worry. Can we ride down the driveway today?"

Over the course of the two weeks since her Willow Art creation had been delivered, Vivi had begged Byron to go riding outside of the arena nearly every day.

He smiled to himself, but schooled his face when he turned to face her. "I don't know if you're ready yet."

With a sigh big enough to turn a windmill, Vivi caught Worry and ran his lead rope through the tie ring. She brushed him down and saddled him. Byron watched, but she was careful and didn't make a mistake. She led the gelding to the arena and swung the gate open.

Byron followed her, admiring the way her Wranglers molded to her butt. As she checked her cinch one last time and started to mount, he cleared his throat. "I need to check on some heifers in the south pasture. Want to come along?"

Vivi turned with a squeal and hurried over to him. "You mean it?" When he nodded, she pulled him into a hug. "Thanks, Byron."

He no longer needed to help her mount and was kind of sorry for that. He'd have to find another way to help her do things. A thought occurred to him that made him smile. A little kiss couldn't hurt anything, could it? She had slept at his house after all.

He put that thought away for another day. When it came right down to it, he was a bit afraid to move this relationship or whatever it was to a more serious level.

Byron swung the gate open and let Vivi ride through. The horses picked their way down to the creek bed. It ran full all summer with runoff from irrigating, but was dry as a bone this time of year.

Clouds threw shadows across the ground and kept a nip in the air. Leafless trees stretched their branches to the sky and a murder of crows scolded them for invading their territory.

"How much land does Micah own?"

"As far as you can see. It will take us over four hours to ride this pasture." He gestured with his arm. "And this is just the winter holding pen for this bunch."

She nodded, apparently speechless. Pulling out her phone, she snapped pictures as they rode.

They'd been riding for over an hour, and Vivi had taken at least a hundred photos when she looked at her phone. "When did we lose phone service?"

"About a quarter mile from the house."

"What happens if someone gets hurt out here? Can you call for help?" The worry in her eyes had him wanting to comfort her.

"I make sure someone always knows where we're going and when we're expected back." He punched her arm lightly. "If I get hurt, you can ride to the top of that hill and use your phone." He pointed to a hill a few miles away.

"Clear over there?" She chewed her lip. "Please don't get hurt."

"I'm not going to get hurt. I do this for a living. I'm a professional." Byron chuckled at her concern. His dad used to be worried as hell he'd get hurt playing football, but only because he'd be out of the game. He wasn't used to someone caring what happened to him if it didn't get them something.

"Promise?"

"Promise." They rode in silence for a while enjoying the views and the meadowlark's songs. Vivi's concern confused him on one hand and pleased him on the other, and he had to control the smile that wanted to spread across his face.

"I know you're from Texas, but not much else. Where did you go to college?" Vivi was relaxed and rode with her reins held loosely.

"What makes you think I went to college? What makes you think I even graduated high school? I'm just a ranch hand." He wasn't sure he wanted to get into his past, but it seemed when Vivi asked he always said more than he'd intended.

She snorted. "Give me a break. You're one of the most intelligent people I've ever met, and let me tell you, I've been around smart people all my life."

When he just stared at her, she continued. "They were all intelligent, but some of them didn't have common sense enough to pour water out of a boot." Her smile brightened her face, and she gave a soft laugh.

"Pour water out of a boot? Where'd you hear that expression? That an old Massachusetts saying?"

Her smile widened. "I googled it. When I decided to come west, I googled lots of western saying so I'd fit in and don't change the subject." She shifted in her saddle and turned part way to stare at him. "College?"

"I went to Penn State." Byron settled his gaze on the

group of cows in the distance. They were the first calf heifers due to calve in November. He made a quick count to make sure they were all there. Satisfied, he turned back to Vivi. "Any more questions?"

"What did you study?"

Vivi's green down coat intensified the color of her eyes. She was smart, sweet, and pretty, and she scared the crap out of him. He jerked his gaze back to the cattle. Quit mooning over her and answer the question. "Football with a minor in business management and math."

"My brother loved math." The words were almost a whisper as she stared off into the distance. When she turned her attention back to him, the usual humor was gone from her gaze. "I studied Physics, and Sebastian was a mathematics genius. I've never been to a football game. Father didn't think it was worth the time. I have watched some on TV, but I can't tell what they're doing. Is there a game around here we could watch?"

He hadn't been to a football game since the day he'd quit college, but he'd heard Micah talk about the local high school. "East Hope High School has an eight man team. They play the other small towns around here. Micah would know when they play again."

The smile that had disappeared when she'd been lost in thought came back with a bang. "If you wouldn't mind, I'd love to see one."

Without a second thought he agreed. When had he become the good guy? In the four years he'd been at the ranch, he could count on one hand the social functions he'd attended.

"So, you have a degree in business management?" She was determined if nothing else.

Might as well get this out. Byron knew if he told her he didn't want to talk about his past, she'd drop the subject, but he'd kept this bottled up inside for so long, it was freeing to tell someone. Besides, Vivi wasn't staying. She'd soon forget all about him and his problems. "I didn't graduate."

"Why?" Simple question. Not so simple answer.

"Dad wanted a football star for a son. At the end of my junior year, my best friend was hurt during a scrimmage. When I tackled him, I broke his back."

"You didn't do it on purpose, did you?" Her eyes never wavered from his, and her concern covered him like a down blanket.

"No!" The word came out sharper than he'd intended. He lowered his voice. "No, I didn't, but if I could hurt him, I could hurt someone else."

"That makes sense."

"I kept trying to tell the old man I didn't want to play, but when the pro scouts started following me, he was relentless. The only reason he cared whether I flunked out or not, was whether I could continue to be a football star. He was embarrassing. Glad handing the alumni. Brown nosing the scouts."

She reached across the space between their horses and touched his arm. When he met her eyes, she pulled back her hand and waited.

Byron thought back to those days. Quitting school was one of the hardest and easiest things he'd ever done. "So the middle of my senior year, I walked away."

"I would have never been strong enough to do that." Her statement was made without the derision his family had voiced or the desperation of his coach.

"Don't know about strong. I quit." The sound of the word his father had spit at him when he was leaving home still rang in his mind. "I quit and threw away a probable job in the NFL. My dad's dream."

~-~

"But not yours." Vivi could see the struggle in Byron's expression. She wasn't sure exactly how long it had been since he'd quit and disappointed his family, but Byron sure hadn't come to terms with it yet. "You don't owe your life to your father. If he wants to have an NFL, whatever that is, in his family, let him play."

Byron barked out a laugh. "My dad is five feet ten inches and weighs one hundred and eighty-five pounds. I get my size from my maternal grandfather."

"And he'd have to be as big as you to play this game?"

"In a word, yes." Byron stepped down from his horse. They'd reached the gate at the ranch and while he opened the gate, Vivi slowly dismounted. "If it's okay with you, I'll walk a while. Long ride." She gave him a sheepish grin. "So your father wanted a football star and you wanted what?"

He opened the gate and closed it after they'd passed through. They were about a half-mile from the barn so they walked side by side. "I wanted to be a cowboy. I'd always wanted to be a cowboy from the moment I spent the weekend on a friend's ranch and rode my first horse."

Vivi watched him stroke the colt's neck from ears to shoulders as he talked. She wanted to ask him to do that to her, but caught herself. They were talking about important things now and she needed to be an adult. But damn, watching the movement of Byron's big hands sent chills down her spine and heated her belly.

She brought herself back to the conversation. "Couldn't you do both?"

"Not according to my dad. He thought riding was a waste of time. Besides, I didn't want to beat up guys on the football field any more. After a while it seemed counterproductive."

"What do you mean?"

"When you train a horse, you work toward making a better animal, responsive and kind. On the field, I just worked to hit the other guy harder and put him out of the game. Not productive." He hesitated. "Dad didn't see it that way."

They'd reached the barn and worked together to put

the animals away.

Vivi hung up the bridles while Byron put the saddles on the racks. She took a deep breath. She could either go to the ranch house for dinner like always or— If she left things up to Byron, they might be buddies forever. "What do you have in your fridge?"

He looked up, confused. "What?"

"I'm offering to cook you dinner." She took his hand and pulled him toward his house. "That's not entirely true. I can only cook a couple of things. If you have what I can cook, I'll cook you dinner. So, what do you have in your fridge?"

Byron strode toward his bungalow, now pulling her. "We'll find something. What can you cook?"

"I can microwave almost anything, and I'm good at cereal and sandwiches."

Working beside Byron in his miniscule kitchen, Vivi felt more at home than she ever had in Massachusetts surrounded by her family.

It turned out the only thing he had that she could cook was salad. She set to work on making a masterpiece while Byron grilled steaks.

As they enjoyed the meal, it was Byron's turn to ask questions. "Do you feel like telling me what happened to your brother?"

The bite of steak in her mouth suddenly lost its appeal. She forced herself to finish chewing and swallow. Draining the bottle of Coors, she tried to slow the rapid beating of her heart.

"It was the beginning of our senior year of college. We were on our way to register. Mother and Father were with us, like always, because, I guess, Father couldn't trust us to take suitable classes." She stood and grabbed two more beers from the fridge then put one back. The Fireball incident was still clear in her mind, and despite being an easy drunk, she wasn't stupid.

"I think we've already concluded he was an asshole."

Byron waited until she nodded. "Please continue."

She handed him the beer. Picking up her fork, she stood beside the table, playing with what was left of the salad. "We'd registered, and were going out to dinner to celebrate. I'd dropped the folder containing my registration papers and stopped to pick them up when a young man drove up over the curb and hit them, all three of them." She sat dry eyed as she remembered. During the last years, she'd cried all of her tears, but it didn't stop the painful memories. "He'd been texting his girlfriend."

Byron took her hand and pulled her onto his lap. He was warm and solid and everything she needed at that moment. She needed a distraction, and Byron was the best one she could think of.

As she put her hands on his cheeks, his stubble tickled her palms. Looking into his eyes, she tried to find pity, but it wasn't there. Just concern. "Sebastian was killed instantly. Mother lived long enough for the paramedics to get her to the hospital."

"And your dad?"

"He lived for another year in a wheel chair, demanding as ever." She leaned in and kissed Byron. Just a brush of her lips over his, really, but the feeling shot through her to her core. She pulled back. "That was a good thing. If he'd died too, I'd have quit college. Instead, I took online courses while I took care of him."

Byron ran his hand through her hair, stroking her like the horse. "But the guy didn't hit you, did he? You weren't hurt?"

"No, the car just missed me. If I hadn't stopped…"

"Thank God you did!" Byron stiffened and pulled her a little closer.

"But if I hadn't been looking down, maybe I could have grabbed Sebastian, pulled him back. I can't forget the sight. He was so broken." She laid her head on his shoulder and let a few tears fall. They weren't all gone after all. "Maybe I could have saved him."

"This wasn't your fault."

"The doctors said Sebastian didn't feel a thing. They told me to be thankful for that. I didn't feel very thankful." She felt his strong arms wrap around her and pull her close. For her father, any type of emotion was a sign of weakness, and she craved Byron's touch. "When I went to visit Father in the hospital after the funeral, his first words were, "The time for crying is past. Get me a nurse." Like losing Mother and Sebastian was some kind of inconvenience.

Vivi brushed the tears off her cheeks then brushed her lips on Byron's again. She was done telling the terrible story of her life, done living in the past. Finding her own kind of happiness, no matter for how long was her goal.

But what did she do next? Her experience in seducing someone was limited. A slight smile curved her lips as they pressed against his. Her new life motto was when in doubt, jump in with both feet.

As a scientist, she'd been good at research and reading, and during her quest for freedom and happiness, she'd read several romance novels. She decided to mimic the passionate kisses she'd read about. She needn't have worried. When she pressed her lips against his, Byron took over.

The rush of sensation threatened to overwhelm her, but she'd promised herself to never back away from a new experience again. Her heart raced, and a wonderful warmth spread down from her belly to her thighs.

At the silky slide of his tongue against hers, she readjusted so she straddled his legs. *O, holy cats!*

Byron put his hands under her butt and pulled her against him. The friction was doing amazing things to her body, and she strained to get closer. He stood and carried her to the bed, never breaking the kiss.

The bed creaked as he laid her down then rolled so they were facing each other. One big rough finger ran down her cheek before moving along her neck. When his hand cupped her breast, he stopped. "Are you sure about this?" he asked, his voice husky.

She nodded. She hadn't been sure about much in her life, but she was sure about this man.

He rolled to his back and pulled her on top of him, returning to the kiss. When she pulled away breathless, she smiled at him. "You'll have to tell me what to do, what you like."

Byron stiffened. "You have done this before, right?"

Damn! She should have kept her mouth shut. Her inexperience was showing as if she'd posted in neon lights. She'd wanted to give him everything he wanted. Hadn't wanted to make a mistake, and now he knew. "I have done this before."

Bryon sat up, shifting her to the side and tucking her under his arm. "But not a lot?"

"No, not a lot." Maybe he wasn't totally repulsed by her lack of knowledge of sex.

"I kind of need to know this stuff, Vivi. Have you had sex before?" He turned his intimidating stare on her.

But he didn't let go. And besides, she didn't do intimidation any more. "I prefer to use the term making love." She brushed her hair off her face and pasted a smile on her face. Fake it to make it.

"Calling it sex or making love is not the point. Are you a virgin?"

All her bravado deserted her like the fake emotion it was. "There was no chance of doing anything while my father was alive. Since then—I haven't had the most rewarding experiences."

"Did someone hurt you?" Byron tilted her chin up so she had to look him in the eye.

Vivi sighed. "No, no one hurt me. I was looking for emotion, a connection to someone. They weren't." She placed a hand on his cheek. "I hadn't found the right man. Until now."

Byron shifted on the bed.

She tried to stand. He was going to reject her because she didn't know what she was doing. The few times she attempted sex had been fast and unrewarding, at least for her.

This becoming an experienced woman was harder to become than she'd thought.

CHAPTER NINE

Byron pulled her back onto his lap and gently laid her head onto his shoulder. Her silky hair spread across the front of his shirt and her sweet scent wafted up, surrounding him. "What am I going to do with you, Vivi?"

"How about having sex with me? What's wrong with that?"

The chuckle started deep in his chest. The woman had balls, he had to give her that. "Tell you what. How about we make out? Take it one step at a time." And he couldn't believe what had just come out of his mouth. A willing woman in his lap, and he opted for kissing. Not that he didn't like kissing, but the guys on the football team would have called him names for not pushing his advantage.

She lifted her head and looked him in the eye. "It's not that I don't like your kissing, but are you sure?"

"Oh, honey. I'm so sure it hurts."

He'd thought she was a free love hippy girl. Guess he got the free love part wrong, and for some perverse reason that made him happy.

He smiled. "I do believe this is the first time I've discussed the terms of a make-out session. You are a unique woman, Vivi."

"That I am, and don't you forget it."

"Vivi is an unusual name. Is it a nickname?"

"What about the kissing? You said there'd be kissing." She moved closer and began giving him light kisses, one after the other.

Byron deepened the kisses until they were both out of breath. He smoothed her hair behind her ear. "You can't kiss your way out of an answer. Nickname or not?"

"You are a single-minded man, aren't you?" She laid her chin on his chest and looked at him from beneath her lashes. "Viola Margaret Beckett. Sebastian and I were named for characters in Shakespeare's Twelfth Night."

"Viola is pretty. Did your family call you Vivi?"

"Oh, heavens no! My father and mother would have had a fit if I'd gone by a nickname. Most of the time they called me Viola Margaret." She stiffened, her head dropped against his chest and she sighed. "Vivi was Sebastian's pet name for me."

"What was your secret name for him?" Byron traced circles on her back, hoping to calm her.

"Ronnie." When Byron raised his eyebrows in question, she continued. "His middle name was Ronald for Ronald Reagan, my father's hero."

She made a visible little shake and straightened. "Can we stop with the questions? I want to get back to the kissing."

When her lips touched his, fire shot through his veins, and he instantly regretted his kissing-only rule. Her soft little kisses turned hot. His hand found its way to her breast, and she moaned. Her nipple hardened against his palm. He was going to have to be careful, or he'd lose control, and this woman didn't deserve a quickie.

Her lips still touched his lightly. "What's wrong? Where did you go?"

"Oh, I'm right here. Believe me. I don't want to be anywhere else." He grinned at the perplexed look on her face. "Just trying to maintain control."

The look changed to a smile. "You're the first man who's had that problem with me. Most don't see me at all."

"As beautiful as you are, I can't believe that." He was having a hard time keeping his hands off her. He wanted to touch every square inch of her body.

Her smile widened. "You think I'm pretty?"

She had to know what a knock out she was, didn't she? "I think you're more than pretty." This kissing only thing wasn't working. If he didn't get some distance, he'd throw her down on the bed and take her.

Damned inconvenient conscience.

"Since I've changed the way I dress, I've had some men make remarks, but it was obvious what they wanted." Her serious expression made him laugh. She spoke her mind almost without a filter. There wasn't an untruthful bone in her body.

"Don't' kid yourself, Vivi. I want sex," he said. If she could speak her mind, he'd do the same.

"Yes, but I want you, too. That's the difference."

Her simple words went straight to his heart. He slipped his hands beneath her shirt and slowly ran them up her ribcage. She raised her arms, and he pulled the silky garment off her shoulders.

Her bra was as deep purple as the T-shirt, with lacy edges that framed her breasts. He spent a moment just staring. Was there anything that wasn't perfect about her?

He'd been caught up in the beautiful sight when Vivi leaned away and crossed her arms over the breasts, hiding them. The uncertainty he saw when he looked in her eyes stunned him. She dropped her gaze and tried to wiggle away. "I know they aren't very big, and one is smaller than the other." She sucked in a rapid breath and raised her gaze to him. "But they're mine and if you don't like them, I'll just—I'll just…" She glanced around and reached for her shirt.

He put his fingers over the lips. "Stop. They're perfect.

You're perfect. I was just looking." At her tentative smile he slipped a bra strap off her shoulder then kissed the place it had been. "A man can look, right?"

He ran his finger beneath the other strap, and in an instant her breasts were bare in front of him. He leaned in slowly, giving her plenty of time to change her mind. When she didn't move away, he pulled one nipple into his mouth and sucked softly. Her soft moan urged him on and he moved to the other breast.

Vivi wrapped her arms around his neck and pulled his mouth up to hers. The tentative way her tongue slid against his shorted out his brain.

He reached for her zipper and just as he slid it down, a soft knock sounded on the door. "Byron?" Willa's high-pitched voice called through the door. "I need to talk to you." The knock sounded again.

Damn! He bolted upright and twisted so he could see the door. Of course he'd been too wrapped up in Vivi to remember to throw the lock. He couldn't let Willa walk in and see her like this.

Vivi had scrambled off the bed and sat on her knees, trying to pull on her T-shirt. "Darn! Heck! Poop!" Her words were spoken in a whisper, and she probably considered them swearing. He'd have laughed if this weren't such a screwed up situation.

The door rattled. "Byron. Dad says I can go riding with you if you say it's okay."

He twisted the knob and opened the door just far enough to see the little girl's face. "Hey, Willa. I'm a little busy right now. How about in an hour?"

"Okay." She smiled as her always-unruly hair floated in a halo around her head. He started to close the door when she put her hand against it. "Byron?"

"What Willa?" He had to work to make his words sound natural.

She leaned back and forth, trying to see past him. "Can Vivi come with us?"

Vivi appeared at his side, her cheeks pink and laughter in her voice. "Of course I will."

Willa tilted her head as she looked from Byron to Vivi. "Why is your shirt on inside out?"

Without missing a beat, Vivi said, "It's supposed to be that way. It's a fashion statement."

Willa nodded, pulled her lip between her teeth then turned to Byron. "Is Vivi your girlfriend?"

~-~

Vivi still blushed every time she thought of what Willa almost saw. It had been a week, and she still laughed when she remembered how Byron struggled to answer Willa's question.

She couldn't laugh too much though. If she hadn't recently read a romance novel where the heroine had used the fashion statement excuse, she'd have been at a loss for words, too.

Fear and excitement raced alternately through her when she thought of being alone with Byron again. He'd made sure someone else had been with them since their encounter with Willa, but Vivi had come up with a plan.

She watched as he rode toward the hills. Micah had told her where Byron was going. She'd paid attention and now could catch, saddle and ride Worry by herself.

She reveled in the cool fall air and the total silence of riding through the hills. She'd given Byron a half hour's head start. When they'd gotten far enough from the house, she urged Worry into a ground-covering trot.

Byron had worked his horse down a steep ravine and come up on the other side. He'd stopped the colt and looked back. She saw the moment he noticed her.

Vivi waved and turned Worry down the narrow trail.

Byron had dismounted and was waving both arms. She waved back just before he disappeared as she descended the slope. She could hear him calling to her, but couldn't hear the words. She'd be over there soon enough.

The trail got steeper and switched back. Maybe this wasn't a good idea and she stiffened and pulled on the reins. Worry stopped and waited in a spot where the bank rose straight up on one side and nearly straight down on the other.

Vivi made herself relax in the saddle, but kept a tight hold on the reins. Byron's words came back to her. *If you get into trouble to trust Worry.* Even when she stroked his neck he stood like a statue. She sucked in a breath and loosened her grip. She placed her hand on Worry's neck and gave him some slack in the reins.

He stood for another moment then began taking small steps down the steep slope. The animal eased them to the bottom. She was looking for the best place to climb the other side when Byron crashed through the underbrush.

"What the hell are you doing? I told you I'd come to you."

Well, heck, she'd been so proud of herself for remembering Byron's words and very proud of Worry for taking care of her. "I brought you a picnic lunch, but if you don't want it, I'll just go back to the ranch." She turned Worry and started back the way she'd come.

"Wait," Byron called. "Follow me up." When she didn't move, he added, "Please."

The climb to the top was made in silence. When they broke out onto the meadow, she was amazed at the view. Across the ravine toward the house, the cows grazed. The view of the mountains, painted in shades of blue and purple, took her breath away.

Byron stopped and dismounted. "What were you thinking? You can't just go riding wherever you want. It's dangerous." He towered over her, and his overprotective attitude made her grit her teeth.

"I spent most of my life listening to a man put me down. I swore when Father died, I'd never do that again. If you'll show me the safe way back to the ranch, I'll stay out of your way." She stood her ground, although looking as far up as she had to do with Byron probably took away some of her attitude.

Byron took off his hat, wiped his forehead with his sleeve and resettled the straw. He slipped a set of hobbles off his saddle and knelt beside the colt. The he tied the Mecate to a branch, leaving enough slack for the colt to drop his head and graze on the dried grass. When he walked over to where Vivi stood, he hobbled the older horse then took off his bridle.

"Worry won't run away?"

"Not if the other horse stays here." Byron took her hand and led her to a fallen log. He sat down and patted the place beside him. "I'm sorry I yelled. You scared me."

"I let Worry go where he wanted. Just like you said." Vivi couldn't understand what his problem was. She'd done as he'd instructed.

Byron sat with his forearms resting on his thighs, his head hanging. "If you'd gotten scared and tried to turn him around, he could have fallen, taking you with him."

"But you told me what to do. I trust you." She put her hand on his thigh, but resisted the urge to stroke up his leg. "I'm not a stupid airhead. I can follow instructions."

His sigh carried all the weight of his worries. "I don't want you to get hurt."

She did let her hand move up his leg and back down. "I'm okay. I promise to try not to do things to make you crazy, but I'm an adult and I can make decisions for myself. Besides, Worry takes care of me." She grinned. "I'm fine. Are you hungry?"

He nodded but his smile wasn't there.

"Look, I promise to be more careful, but I can't live just so you won't worry."

After retrieving the saddlebags from Worry's back, Vivi pulled a thin blanket from inside and spread it on the ground. She'd made sandwiches, had a small bag of chips and a large plastic bag of Cary's famous chocolate chip cookies.

Maybe she could get him in a sugar coma and have her way with him. The thought made her chuckle, and she looked up to see Byron watching her, his eyes dark and his gaze smoldering. Had he read her thoughts?

She ducked her head, the smile still on her face and unwrapped one of the turkey sandwiches. "I'm not much of a cook, but I can make a mean sandwich."

Byron still watched her as he reached out. His voice was gentle, but his words shocked her. "What are you doing here?"

"Well, uh. The truth?"

"Yes." Byron touched her hand as he took the sandwich, and a jolt ran up her arm.

"I wanted to be alone with you." She felt a blush crawl up her cheeks, but stared him straight in the eye. If he rejected her, that was that, but she wasn't backing down on what she wanted. Life was too short.

He studied her for so long, she thought about climbing on Worry and riding away.

Byron cleared his throat. "One more question."

"Okay." She braced herself. This should be easier. She'd always thought if a woman threw herself at a man, he'd take what she offered. That's what all the books and movies showed.

She wasn't expecting forever. She liked Byron. She did, but she knew he wasn't ready to share his life. He probably never would be ready.

"Why are you standing way over there?" Byron held out his hand.

"I thought I might add a little mystery to our relationship, not throw myself at you the very first thing. Not that we have a relationship." This wasn't going at all like she'd planned. "Just sex. That's what we have. You're my Benefit Friend."

"Friend with benefits?" Byron waited, his hand still out.

She loved the way it felt when Byron took her hand, his

large warm one wrapping around hers. He dropped to the ground and tugged on her until she sat beside him.

"I'm not sure I've ever had a woman come straight out and ask for sex. You're sure?"

The humor in his voice turned her on. Everything about Byron Garrett turned her on. She crawled into his lap and straddled his legs, facing him. "Sure as a windy day in March."

"Another one of your Google sayings?"

"Yes," she said, her voice a whisper.

Byron slid his hand beneath her jacket and shirt to the bare skin of her back. He ran a finger up her spine, slowing over each vertebra. He stroked her skin with one hand and cupped the back of her head with the other.

When his lips touched hers, Vivi sighed. Out here, nothing could interrupt them. She ran her hands over his biceps and up to his shoulders. Winding her arms around his neck, she pulled him close. The soft snort barely registered in her subconscious as she fell into Byron's kisses.

A loud snort seconds later caught their attention. Both horses stood stiff, their heads in the air, their ears perked in the same direction.

Byron scrambled to his feet, almost dropping her in his haste. "Aw, shit!" The colt pulled back. The branch broke with a crack just as Byron caught the tail end of the Mecate. Despite the hobbles, the colt tried to run, and it took all of Byron's strength to keep the animal from escaping.

Vivi looked for what had scared the colt and gasped as a dark brown bear stood to his full height.

"Put Worry's reins around his neck, now, and see if you can get the bridle on. Hurry." Byron struggled to get his colt under control.

The bear stood still, probably wondering what all the fuss was about, then dropped to all fours and crashed through the brush into the ravine.

The colt trembled but calmed with the bear gone. He wasn't relaxed by any means. Byron crooned to the animal, trying to reassure him. Worry watched until the bear was out of sight, flicked his ears a couple of times then dropped his head.

Vivi managed to get the bridle on him and led her horse over the Byron. "Wow, I've never seen a bear. How cool."

"Wouldn't have been cool if we'd have had to walk back."

CHAPTER TEN

Lester Charters opened his email account to find yet another message from Viola. He thought briefly of deleting it without opening it, but Viola was a tenacious little thing, and she'd just write back.

Dear Mr. Charters,

I just wanted to keep you apprised of what's happening in my search for a suitable property for my art studio. I'm sending you the listings for two possible places, one in Bend, Oregon and one in the resort community of Crooked River Ranch. Quite honestly, neither one seems perfect but they're the closest I've found so far. I'll look at them next week. If nothing comes up, I'll expand my search parameters into Washington and Idaho.

Sincerely,
Viola Beckett

He opened the attachments. The property in Bend was so run down he was surprised she'd even look at it. It would take a small fortune to fix up. The price of the Crooked River Ranch property almost made him choke. Not that she couldn't afford it. Her grandfather had left her a large fortune, but he had the money tied up, working for her—and for him.

He thought for a moment then typed his reply.

My dear Viola,

Not to dash your hopes, but I'd advise against the Bend property no matter how good of a bargain the realtor says it is. The Crooked River property is beautiful. After you visit it why don't you send me a list of the pros and cons you see with the house and surrounding property. We'll go through them together and make sure it is the place for you and your beautiful art. Buying your first home is a big decision, and we want you to have the perfect place.

Take care and I'll talk to you soon.

Sincerely,

Lester Charters

~-~

Twice, he'd had Vivi in his arms, willing and warm then something or someone had interrupted them. Who had he pissed off?

He turned to find Vivi with Worry bridled. "Good old Worry. I'm not sure if there's anything that could upset him.

"He's amazing. Will your young horse be this quiet when he gets older?"

"They're all different. He'll get better, but he's pretty high strung. I doubt if he's another Worry." Byron bent down and worked the hobbles loose.

"You said Worry was a good horse the first time I rode him. He's more than good, he's the best."

"We need to head back. I don't think that bear will bother us. They're usually happy to leave people alone if we leave them alone, but he's spooked this colt, and I sure don't want to meet the animal on the narrow ravine trail. We'll have to take the long way home."

Handing the reins to Byron, Vivi gathered the lunch things.

It didn't help his out of control libido to watch her bend, her cute little ass outlined in the denim. If he didn't get his hard on to go away, it was going to be an uncomfortable ride home.

Vivi folded the blanket and stowed the food in the saddlebags. She took the reins and mounted her horse like she'd done it all her life.

Hard to imagine that just two months ago she'd never ridden. Byron felt a jolt of pride in her determination and drive. When Vivi set her mind to something nothing stopped her.

He shortened one rein just in case the colt decided running off was his best option then swung into the saddle. He reached over and took Vivi's hand. Just another touch of her soft skin to keep him going until they could be alone. It didn't last more than a second before the colt danced away.

Vivi asked one question after the other about the bear.

"I haven't seen a bear for several years. Must be a young one that's moved into the area."

"Won't they hurt the cows?"

The worry on her face almost made Byron smile. She was as soft hearted as they came. "ON very rare occasions, they might hurt a calf, but like all mothers, mama cows will defend their babies with their lives."

Her voice dropped to a whisper, and if he'd been any farther away, he wouldn't have heard. "Not all mothers."

She was right about that.

When he caught her eye, she looked away and pointed. "How long does it take to get back to the ranch?"

Vivi asked about other wildlife in the area, how his colt was doing, and if he'd liked his sandwich. She kept up the barrage of questions, only being quiet when he had to ride far enough ahead of her that she'd have to shout.

He'd tried to bring up the subject of her mother once, and she'd shut him down. Dear old mom must be off limits. He was surprised. She'd talked pretty regularly about her dad, the asshole.

By the time they reached the barn, Byron could see that Vivi was dragging. He offered to take care of Worry, but she wouldn't have it.

They were walking toward the ranch house after putting the horses away, when they saw a strange car. Cary and a woman stood by the steps, and as soon as Cary saw them, she waved them over.

"Vivi, this is Marissa Cole, the realtor I told you about. Marissa, this is Vivi Beckett and Byron Garrett."

The woman looked out of place on the ranch. Her cream-colored pantsuit wouldn't last long in the dirt. She shook Vivi's hand then turned to Byron. He'd seen the look before. Her gaze wandered over him from his feet to his head, with a stop in between.

"So nice to meet you Mr. Garrett. Will you be looking at the property too?" Her smile was intended to be friendly, but her expression made Byron think of a coyote with a jackrabbit in its sight.

He looked at Vivi. "Property?" The word came out harsher than he'd intended, and he could see the confusion on Vivi's face.

"Ms. Cole thinks she's found a home and property that would be perfect for my art studio. I'd love it if you could come look at it with us." She reached out tentatively and placed her hand on his arm.

And once again, he had proof positive that he was a fool. His home was the little bungalow on the Circle W. No woman with as much going as Vivi would settle for that. Of course she was looking for a place of her own, and she should. Her talent was remarkable. He cleared his throat and tried to erase the frown from his face. "I've got to work. Have fun."

He headed back to the barn and found the kittens playing in the aisle. He scooped up the calico and rubbed her beneath the chin. "Looks like it's just you and me, kid."

~_~

Vivi had searched the barn and out buildings when she'd arrived home, but could find no sign of Byron. The look on his face when he found out she was looking for property had confused her. She had mentioned that, hadn't she?

He'd walked away without giving her a chance to explain. Even with the realtor waiting, she should have gone after him, but the manners drilled into her by her parents won out.

The property search hadn't gone as well as the realtor had predicted. Ms. Cole chattered all the way to Bend, telling Vivi how perfect each of the properties would be for her business. "Don't let the condition of the Bend property scare you off. All it needs is a little TLC, and I know just the contractor. You could remodel and make it exactly what you want."

"The pictures look like it's awfully run down."

When they'd gotten there, Vivi found the pictures had been right. The house was a tear down, and the property was at the end of a narrow dirt road, way off the beaten path. Even fixed up, it would be hard for customers to find her.

The house and acreage at the Crooked River development was the opposite. It was an elegant four thousand square foot house, but had no studio space. Neither place was even remotely appropriate.

During the drive back to the ranch, Ms. Cole continued to use every opportunity to convince Vivi one of the places would be perfect.

Vivi found Cary in the kitchen, making cupcakes with Willa and Rodie. After talking to each of the kids, she asked, "Do you know where Byron is?"

"He took the rest of the day off. Said he had something to do in town."

Vivi could see that Cary was curious, but this was between her and Byron. "Thanks. See you kids later."

Vivi walked to Byron's bungalow and sat in the old rocker. The light changed from bright to golden until the sun dipped below the horizon. She curled up on his bed to wait.

The sound of the door opening woke her. Byron filled the doorway, a plastic grocery sack in each hand, and she scrambled to her feet. "I've been waiting."

He looked her up and down and grunted once before heading into the kitchen and putting the canned goods away. The man she knew had disappeared, and the angry silent man she'd first met was back.

"We need to talk." She tried to get in front of him, but he bent down and began putting stuff in the refrigerator.

"Little late for that." His voice was gruff, the kind warm tone she was used to completely gone.

"Byron, I just went to look at a couple of places. Neither of them is going to work."

"But you are looking."

She reached out to touch his shoulder then she hesitated, not sure why. He wouldn't hurt her. Not physically. She stepped closer and laid her hand on his arm. "Please talk to me."

The hurt and anger in his expression stunned her. "Nothing to talk about. I get it. You said you wanted to be friends. What you really wanted was a fuck buddy with no strings." His face was hard, and his eyes cold as he watched her.

His choice of words hurt. She'd never thought of sex in those terms, especially not with him. "The realtor found out I was an artist and suggested looking for a studio. Before I knew it, she'd set up appointments at these two places."

Anger, hot and hard, replaced the hurt when he stared at her. "And I don't fuck men. I make love." As the words came out of her mouth, she realized how stupid they sounded. She really hadn't done much of either.

She'd never used that word before and determined not to use the ugly thing again. Tears burned behind her eyes, and she blinked to keep them back. No way was she crying in front of Byron.

She headed for the door before she compromised her morals anymore. Besides, she couldn't hold back the tears for much longer.

Were all men single-minded and domineering? She'd thought Byron was different. Disappointment flooded her emotions. He wasn't different after all. She grabbed the handle and jerked the door open. Striding toward the house, she pasted a pleasant look on her face.

Having Cary and Micah feel sorry for her wouldn't change a thing. She'd pack in the morning and continue her search for her place in the world. She'd felt at home here, but obviously she'd created a fantasyland.

She'd almost reached the porch when she heard Byron behind her. His hand closed around her upper arm. She saw Willa watching them through the window and knew she couldn't make a scene, so she turned to him, a brittle smile on her face. "Willa is watching." Her words hissed in anger.

Byron let go, but stepped closer. His expression softened, but the disappointment remained. "I don't want to fight with you. I'm sorry I overreacted. Maybe I expected too much. Aw, hell. This isn't coming out right." He ran his hands through his hair and stared at the toes of his boots. "I'm just not sure this is the right thing to do."

"Not the right thing to do? What, being friends or seeing if there's something more between us." She straightened and jammed her hands on her hips. "What ever you think is best for you, I'll go along with, and I'll own any mistakes I make. What I won't do is be punished for something I didn't do."

"Why didn't you tell me you were going to move so soon?" He'd stiffened too, but she could handle an honest question.

"I don't know that I am. It all came up so fast. Ms. Cole was supposed to contact me when she had appropriate properties instead of showing up with the appointments already made. I was going to get your opinion on them and see if you'd come look at them with me."

His shoulders relaxed slightly, but his expression remained grim. "Okay, I did overreact. I'm sorry."

"You're forgiven." She sensed something was still bothering him. "What else is wrong?"

He shrugged. "Doesn't change the fact that you're leaving. Probably for the best though. I'm not looking for anything long term."

Or anything short term or anything at all. He was right. If this whatever it was between them had progressed any farther, it would be much harder when he decided to break it off.

And what was it? Raw sexual attraction? The term in relation to how she saw herself almost made her giggle. When she saw the look on his face, the humor died before it was born. "You're right. I think it best to just remain friends. If you even want that."

CHAPTER ELEVEN

What was it his grandfather used to say? Beware of what you wish for. You might get it. Byron hadn't minded his life before Vivi. He'd thought he'd liked it. Peace, tranquility and solitude were the things he'd been looking for. So why had all the color gone out of his world?

He was surrounded by shades of gray. He knew he was better off in the long run to stay alone, but for once in his life, he was questioning his choices.

Vivi hadn't come riding since their last discussion. As much as he'd grumbled in the beginning, he missed her bright outlook and desire to learn everything.

Without thinking, he caught Worry and saddled him. She had said she wanted to remain friends, so what was wrong with friends going for a short ride?

Byron strode to the house. He hesitated before knocking. Get it together for shit's sake. He was just asking her to go riding, not to get married. Why was his heart hammering in his chest?

He rapped three times. Through the heavy oak door, he could hear Willa and Rodie racing to answer. "Hi, Byron. Want to come play with me?" Even though nerves had him on edge, he couldn't help but smile at the little boy. "Sure, what are we playing?" He'd always had a soft spot for kids.

"My match-em cards." The little boy grabbed Byron's hand and pulled him to the coffee table in front of the couch.

A jumble of small cards were scattered on the table, face down with a Toy Story logo visible on each one. Rodie plopped down beside the table. "You can sit on the couch cause you're big."

As Byron settled onto the over-stuffed leather sofa, he asked, "How do you play match-em cards?"

Willa dropped to sit beside her brother. "You're supposed to match the cards or you have to put them back, but Rodie doesn't know how to do that. We just take turns choosing cards and keeping them."

Rodie bounced up and down. "I gets to go first." He picked up a card with Buzz Lightyear on the front then one with Slinky Dog. The little boy hugged the cards to his chest and grinned. "Your turn."

Byron chose two cards that didn't match either but he played along. He looked at Willa. "How do we know who wins?"

"Well, if Rodie accidently picks up a matched pair, he thinks he wins. If not, who ever has the most cards wins." She took her turn. "This is his favorite game."

When all the cards had been picked up, Rodie counted each pile with just a couple of mistakes. Willa had the most by one card and much to Byron's surprise the little boy hugged his sister and scampered away.

"Do you know if Vivi is here?"

Willa tilted her head as she studied him. "Did you have a fight?"

Out of the mouths of babes. "Not really. Just a difference of opinion."

"You had a fight. She's been sad." Willa studied him with an air too old for her twelve years. "I'll go get her. Don't hurt her feelings again." With that, she disappeared.

Oh, shit. Even the kids were on to him. What if Vivi didn't want to see him? Maybe she'd ask Willa to send him away. He'd been a few months from becoming a safety in the NFL, and now he was scared of a tiny, kindhearted woman. *Suck it up, Garrett.*

He heard the murmur of voices and footsteps coming down the stairs. Standing, he prepared to meet Vivi.

The novice cowgirl in Wranglers and boots was gone, replaced with the colorful, wistful hippy girl he'd first seen. Even with the flowing skirt and bright colored necklace and bracelets, how had he ever thought she was a starry-eyed dreamer?

She didn't meet his gaze, and he thought for a moment she'd leave him standing there. Willa stood behind Vivi, her eyes locked on his.

"Willa, would you leave us alone for a minute?" Byron watched as the girl thought over his request. With a nod in his direction, she disappeared into the kitchen.

Vivi hadn't moved. She stood with her arms crossed below those luscious breasts. Her eyes were focused on her shiny pink sandals. Even though he waited several minutes, she didn't look up. She wasn't making this easy on him, but he didn't deserve easy.

"I haven't seen you around for a few days. Everything all right?" Byron longed to see her smile.

"I've been busy." No smile there and he realized he'd never seen her remain straight-faced for longer than a few minutes, even when he'd been at his worst to her in the beginning.

"You missed your riding lessons." He hoped her love of horses would break the ice. "Worry asked where you were."

When she just looked at him, dread filled his gut. He dropped onto the couch. She turned to go and he jumped to his feet. "Would you come out on the porch with me?"

She raised her gaze, not a flicker of interest on her face. "Why?"

"We need to talk." He wiped a sleeve across his forehead. "You said you wanted to remain friends. I'd like that."

There was no expression on her face, and the only indication she was tense was the soft tapping of her toe against the red fir floor. "Friends?"

"Yes. I want us to be friends." He wanted so much more than that, but if he asked for what he really wanted, she'd break his heart when she left.

He saw the exact moment she forgave him. Her shoulders lowered, and her jaw relaxed. She walked out onto the porch and sat in one of the oversized Adirondack chairs, leaning back against the colorful cushion. "You want to be friends." She folded her hands in her lap and turned her bright blue eyes on him. "Just friends?"

"Well, yeah." He sat carefully on one of the other chairs before leaning back and stretching out his legs. "We can go back to the way we were before, right?"

She stood and moved to the railing. When she faced him, her expression was grim. "No, we can't."

Now he was confused. He'd thought she was onboard for the friend thing.

"We will be polite to each other, and give each other a hand when we need it, and I will probably take a riding lesson from you once in a while, but we won't go back to the way things were."

Byron had watched Vivi laugh, he'd watched her almost cry, he'd watched her be kind to the children and animals, but he'd never seen her as serious as she was standing there looking at him like he was a bug on a stick.

Vivi's beautiful eyes were filled with determination. "I lived much of my life, tiptoeing around, trying to not make my father mad. I can't do that with you. Friends don't treat each other that way."

~-~

Unease had gripped Vivi as she drove the hours to Leavenworth, Washington, this time, meeting a realtor that wasn't Ms. Cole. The trip with the first realtor had been a monumental waste of time, and Vivi wasn't giving the woman another chance. She'd asked around and found a man with a great reputation for being honest and knowledgeable.

The property had looked good online, but she'd been fooled before. She'd mentioned the trip to Byron, but didn't ask him to go. Leavenworth was farther from her new friends than she'd wanted, but it was a perfect location for her business.

The online pictures and description hadn't done the property justice. Three hundred timbered acres was more land than she needed, but the handcrafted log house, built from trees cut on the property, gave her a warm feeling of belonging. The rustic lines and huge beams were something she'd only seen in pictures, but once she'd walked inside, she couldn't imagine living anywhere else.

The white clapboard building tilting ever so slightly to the left might have been an old mercantile. It sat on the edge of the property next to the highway only a half a mile from town. From the looks of it, it hadn't been used for more years than Vivi had been alive, but with a lot of work, it would be a perfect studio. Within walking distance from Leavenworth's main street was an added bonus.

The realtor had been a no-nonsense man in his early fifties who seemed more interested in finding her what she wanted than making a sale. His family had spent three generations living around Leavenworth, and he entertained her with stories of the area. "Let me know if you have any questions or want to look at more property," he'd said as they shook hands at the end of the showing. "Not too many properties like this around here, but I could probably scare up another one or two."

The first large drops of rain plopped onto the windshield as she'd started back toward East Hope, the dark skies mirroring her dark mood. She didn't need to look at more places. The joy of having found the perfect home was dampened by the loss of a dream.

The drive back gave her more time than she'd wanted to think. This was the end. Byron wouldn't leave the Circle W and she couldn't be a burden to Micah and Cary any longer. They'd been good friends, had helped her more than she'd expected, but it was time for her to get on with her life.

Hoping for a committed relationship with Byron was a pipe dream. She could feel herself falling in love with him, but he hadn't even hinted that he'd wanted more.

She'd left the eastern Unites States to make her own way. Somehow she'd gotten waylaid in a tiny town and lost her heart to a big, kind cowboy.

As she sat in front of the ranch house, she watched the raindrops stream down the windshield. The six plus hour drive had exhausted her and hopelessness weighted her heart down. Maybe it would be easier if she just packed up and left without talking to Byron. She laid her head on the steering wheel. That would be the coward's way out, and if nothing else, she wasn't a coward.

The sun had set. Byron should be in his bungalow. Before she could change her mind, she ran through the rain to his tiny porch.

The sound of her knuckles meeting the weathered wood of the door echoed through the silent evening. A chair scraping the scarred wooden floor.

Reaching up, she wiped a drop from her cheek. The desire to turn and run was overwhelming, but made herself stand her ground.

Byron swung the door open, and she saw the smile spread across his face. They'd been cordial in the days since Byron came to the house and offered to be her friend. She didn't want a friend. She wanted Byron to love her as much as she loved him.

That wasn't going to happen.

When Byron saw her standing outside the door, he swung it open wide. "You must be freezing. Go stand by the stove."

Vivi hurried to the small potbellied stove, held her hands over the top and let the warmth sink into her skin. When she turned to face him, it was all she could do to smile. This was the beginning of good-bye. She'd see him in the weeks it would take to finalize the purchase of the Leavenworth property, but after the discussion tonight, nothing would be the same.

She'd spent countless hours imagining what life with Byron would be like. A life that wouldn't happen, no matter how hard she tried.

"I need to tell you something."

Byron dragged one of the oak kitchen chairs closer to the fire, but she remained standing.

"I found a place."

He nodded and motioned to the chair.

Well, what the heck. She didn't want to be rude. As Vivi sat down, she tried to relax, but couldn't stop winding the turquoise and silver ring around her index finger.

Byron watched her, waiting.

She'd rehearsed her speech on the drive back to the Circle W. "It's in Leavenworth, Washington. Three hundred acres with a beautiful house. But the thing that attracted me is the shop. It's perfect for my studio." This was harder than she'd thought it would be, and Byron wasn't helping. If he'd get mad, she could stomp out. If he begged her to stay—no, he wouldn't do that, but if he acted like he'd miss her at all, she was afraid she'd reconsider.

He picked up her hand and looked into her eyes. "You think this is the perfect place?"

"Yes, I think so." It wasn't. No place would be perfect without Byron, but the small town property was probably as close as she'd get. "Leavenworth is a tourist town and artist's colony. It should be a great area to base my studio."

"If this is what you want, go for it."

Vivi sighed. In the back of her mind, she'd held out the hope that Byron would do something. Ask her to stay, offer to go with her—even offer to go check out the property as a friend.

His sad smile almost brought tears to her eyes. "I'm happy for you."

It really was over then.

Byron walked to the sink filled with dishes and started the water running. He kept his back to her.

"Want to go look at it with me?" Where had those words come from? She was a glutton for punishment. Way to set herself up for another disappointment. "You don't have to. Never mind."

He stood, looking over his shoulder, his hands still in the soapy water. His gaze wandered over her, finally stopping on her lips. He looked into her eyes and nodded.

"You do?" Her stupid heart raced with excitement, and she couldn't wipe the smile off her face. So much for playing it cool. "When would be a good time for us to go?"

He pulled a towel off the horseshoe rack beside the sink and wiped his hands. "It's supposed to rain for the next few days. How about tomorrow?"

"In the rain?" She didn't have a raincoat.

"Little rain never hurt anyone." He lifted the top of an old trunk and pulled out a bright yellow slicker. Shaking it out, he draped it across her shoulders. He was so close, if she stood on her tiptoes, she could kiss him. His eyes burned into hers and he tugged her closer with the lapels of the coat.

Vivi swore she stopped breathing, but as her eyes drifted shut in anticipation of the kiss, he stepped away.

~-~

Vivi didn't sleep much that night. Would he like the

place or tell her it was all wrong? She was dressed several hours before they were to meet and was standing on his porch at six a.m. the next morning.

"Burnin' daylight," he said as he came out the door, sliding his arms into his slicker. "Let's go see your new home."

Vivi stuffed her arms into the sleeves of the rubber coat he'd given her the night before. It took three rolls before her fingers peeked out of the ends. The hood covered her face, and she had to hold it back with her hands, but she'd be dry.

The drive back to Leavenworth seemed shorter as they talked about inconsequential things that had happened to each of them since they'd become just friends. The old easiness they'd had was gone, but at least Byron was talking again.

She directed him to the address. The house sat back from the highway, hidden by a row of pine trees and the clapboard building. "I think it's locked, but we can look through the windows. They dashed beneath the dripping cottonwood trees to the front porch. Dark woodwork was visible through the windows. Vivi found her first impression had been right on. She loved this house.

They made their way through tall grass to the backyard. The back porch ran the full length of the house and overlooked a pasture. Beyond that was a cornfield. There were no close neighbors, and the area was silent except for the sound of the rain. To the south, she could just see the first building of town.

Byron climbed the back steps and peered into the kitchen. "Kind of a big house for one person."

"I've learned by now that you never know what changes your life will take, and, like the Boy Scouts, it's better to be prepared."

CHAPTER TWELVE

There was another damned email from Viola. He'd gone four years only hearing from the woman when he'd written her and now he was getting correspondence every other week.

He clicked on the message.

Dear Mr. Charters,

I've made an offer on a piece of property in Leavenworth, Washington. I've attached the real estate listing. As you'll see, there is a log home, another old building, a shop and barn and three hundred acres. At this time, I don't need anywhere near that much land, but it's located near the town and in a prime tourist area. I think the extra land would be a good investment. I have enough to make the down payment, but will need to know the procedure for making the final payment.

Please let me know the next step in completing this transaction.
Thank you for your help and advice,
Viola Beckett

He opened the attachment.

What the hell! Two million dollars down the drain for a place so Charlie Beckett's granddaughter could play with twigs? Ludicrous! Charlie's distrust of Viola's father was the reason he'd made Lester the trustee for his estate. Even when Viola's father died, she'd left the management of the fortune to him. He'd had full control of old Charlie's money all these years, and he wasn't about to give up the fortune now.

Dear Viola,

After having looked into the real estate options the Northwest, I'll have to recommend you put off buying anything right now. My sources say the price of land in that area is experiencing a bubble, and if you can have patience, much better bargains will be available in the near future.

Please feel free to call me with any questions you have and we'll work out a plan of action together.

Best,

Lester Charters

The letter sounded reasonable to him, and Viola had been a reasonable girl for most of the time he'd known her, but the last two years, she'd become unpredictable. Understandable with the death of her family, but maybe it was time to put his foot down.

When she'd insisted on making stick figures, he's thought it would be therapy. He'd never seen what she constructed, but sticks?

When she'd wanted to give more than three-quarters of the fortune away to The National Association of the Deaf, he'd convinced her to put it in a trust to be given to deserving non-profits each year. Of course, he managed the trust.

When she set off cross-country alone to find herself, he'd tried to stop her. But would she listen? No!

Now was not the time for Miss Viola Beckett to decide to take control of her fortune. He decided then and there to make a trip to East Hope, Oregon and talk to Viola face to face.

Someone had to inject reality into the fantasy she'd constructed.

~-~

It had been several days since he'd driven to Leavenworth with Vivi, and he still couldn't wrap his head around the fact that she could buy a two million dollar ranch.

Two million dollars cash.

The fact that his father would consider Vivi a catch had given him heartburn. Mother would be ecstatic at the thought of a rich daughter-in-law.

The house was located at least a half of a mile from the highway, which was great for privacy. The rambling log building seemed to have been crafted by a master carpenter, but it had seen years if not decades of neglect. Hand peeled beams and a stone fireplace that took up most of one wall added character to the rooms, but the interior walls needed repairs.

The original building by the road had reminded him of a smaller version of the Walton's house.

He'd held his breath when Vivi had pushed the door to the smaller building open. Not a wall inside was salvageable, but the stained glass window on the front was still intact. Red fir floors seemed solid and had begged to be refinished. If it was salvageable, it was in the perfect location for her studio.

Remodeling an older place had been in the back of his mind for years, and he had a moment of excitement before reality slapped him alongside his head.

What the hell was he thinking? With all the money Vivi had, she could hire the best carpenters, plumbers and even a high-class designer if she wanted. She didn't need him, and he didn't want to be a rich woman's husband.

As much as he'd wanted to prove to her that this was a wrong move, he couldn't. She'd found what she'd been looking for, and she hadn't asked his opinion on the move. She'd made it clear from earlier conversations, that she made her own decisions.

The down payment was sizeable, but she hadn't hesitated. The only thing slowing down the purchase was the inspections, and from what Byron saw, everything was fixable if you had enough money. Looked to him like her decision had been made.

He'd just finished pulling the shoes off of a four-year-old gelding when he heard her talking to someone. For the first time ever, he heard Vivi raise her voice.

She stood by a rental car in the driveway. Her arms were wrapped around her body, whether to protect herself from the man or the wind, he wasn't sure. Her short, wispy skirt danced around her thighs. The heavy knit sweater didn't provide enough warmth for the chilly day.

The bald head of the older man standing beside her shone in the weak fall sunshine. His hands waved as if to reinforce what he said.

Vivi shook her head, walked a few steps away and then turned back. "I disagree." Despite the mildness of her words, the tone was forceful.

He spoke again and whatever he said made Vivi's face flush in anger.

Byron reached them just in time to hear her last words. "Do whatever you need to do. Just know I'll fight you all the way."

The little man climbed into the car and drove carefully away.

Vivi faced away from him, watching the car, but when he touched her shoulder, she whirled and fell into his arms. Her words were muffled by his shirt, but they made him chuckle. "There are times I think you are the only man on the face of the earth that I like. Sometimes I wonder about you, too."

"Which is it today?" He reveled in the weight of her body against his and her sweet scent.

When she raised her head to look at him, her brows were drawn together and her eyes narrowed. She pulled in a deep breath and let it out slowly, her body relaxing a bit. "I don't know."

Byron took her hand and led her to the bungalow. Inside, he lowered her into the rocker, grabbed a bottle of Evan Williams Bourbon and poured her a shot. "Drink this and tell me what's going on."

She took a small sip, made a face then took another. "It's awful going down, but the after effects aren't bad. What is this?"

"Whiskey. Now what did that little man do?" Vivi was smart and kind and if she was this upset, Byron had no doubt she had a valid reason.

Over the next twenty minutes and another shot of whiskey, Vivi filled him in on the trust fund and the man who'd run it for years. "He was a friend of my Grandy. I've always trusted him implicitly. Now he doesn't want me to have any say in how I use my money. He's treating me like I'm a little girl." She tipped back her head and downed what was left in the glass.

When she reached for the bottle, Byron moved it out of her reach. "You've had enough."

"Are you going to treat me like a child, too?"

"Remember the last time you drank? Want a repeat?"

"N-no." She wrapped her arms around her waist and shudder ran through her body.

He put the bottle back in the cupboard and pulled a Coke from the refrigerator. He poured it over ice and handed it to her. "Drink this. It tastes better."

"Thank you." She took a sip and set the glass on the table. "Are there any good attorneys in East Hope, or any attorneys at all?"

He watched as she pushed her honeyed hair behind her ears. The last time she'd had anything to drink they'd ended up here, on the bed, in each other's arms. She licked her lips, and he almost picked her up to begin where they'd left off. If Willa hadn't interrupted them… He banished the thought.

She was moving and he was staying on at the Circle W.

The instant her thoughts turned in the same direction his had gone, her expression changed. Her irises dilated and her breathing quickened. She pushed the soda away and stood. "I should be going." When he nodded, she smiled. "Or not."

And there it was. She was leaving it up to him. For once, could he live in the present, enjoy this woman and have no regrets? Or was he going to let his past rob him of this moment, too?

"Okay, see you later then." She hesitated then turned and started for the door. As her hand touched the knob, he stood.

"Wait. Do you want to stay for a while? We could cook up some steaks." After looking him up and down, she smiled as she unbuttoned her heavy sweater and let it drop to the floor. Strolling to where he stood, she rested her hands against his abs.

He sucked in a breath at her touch. The tight tank top didn't provide much warmth, but Byron had enough heat for both of them.

"I'd like to stay, but not for steaks." Her hands slowly brushed up his torso. She wrapped her arms around his neck. "I'd like to stay for you."

Blood pounded in his ears and lust raced through his veins. He wanted this woman more than he'd wanted anything in his life. She completed him in a way he hadn't known he needed. But he couldn't keep her, he knew that now.

"I think we'd better stick to steaks."

CHAPTER THIRTEEN

Vivi's heart pounded and her cheeks flamed, but she had no one to blame but herself. She'd initiated this, and Byron had shut her down. He'd made it clear that for some reason, he wouldn't take a chance on a long-term relationship. Was it her money that stood in the way?

She screwed up her courage. She'd never get an answer if she didn't ask. "You seemed shocked when I said I could pay cash for the property. Does it bother you that I my grandfather left me some money?"

Byron studied her before he spoke. "It doesn't bother me, but let's be truthful here. It's not some money. If you can pay two million cash for a place, you have a fucking fortune. Just makes me wonder why you're wasting your time with a broke cowboy." His brows knit in a frown, his lips thinned, and he turned his back on her to stir the soup.

"Money has never been a priority to me. It's just a means to an end. If I can buy a place, I can make a home and do what makes me happy." She placed a hand on his shoulder. The need to touch him, connect with him, was overwhelming.

"Easy to do what makes you happy when you have

more money than Bill Gates." He shrugged off her hand and walked to the cupboard, pulling out bowls and glasses. "My father taught me money can't make you happy. It was all he ever thought about, and no matter how much he made, it was never enough."

"A lot of good it does me to have money. I can't get access to it from Mr. Charters." She picked up the spatula and stirred the soup. "He acts like it's his to spend the way he wants."

Byron finally faced her. "How much money do you have?"

Now she blushed. "I'm not really sure. Grandfather made millions on an invention. This is the first time I've ever asked for a large amount. Foolish, I know."

"Do you have statements?"

"Not here, but I have a post office box, and an agency picks up all my mail. They tell me about anything they think is important." Hands on her hips, she stared at him. "I could get them to overnight them to me. Why?"

"Probably nothing, but it bothers me that your Mr. Charters would be this upset about you buying property. It's not like you're buying drugs or wasting it on something frivolous."

She supposed people might look at Byron and see a *broke cowboy* as he'd called himself, but they'd be wrong. He was smart and savvy. She pulled her cell from her pocket and dialed. Within a few minutes, the agency had promised to send all the statements from Charters Asset Management Company to her by overnight mail.

"I'll have them by tomorrow. You don't really think he's up to something, do you?"

"It doesn't hurt to be sure. Soup's ready."

Vivi filled two bowls while Byron poured them each a coke. Before he sat down, he turned the small television to a Seahawks game. There was still an air of tension between them, but the noise of the crowd and commentary helped fill the silence.

Chunks of chicken floated in a savory broth beside homemade noodles. Vivi knew that because her grandmother had always made homemade noodles. "This is really good. I'll have to have Cary teach me to make it."

"Have her teach you how to make her cinnamon apple rolls instead. I could live on them. No wonder Micah married her."

Vivi grinned. "I won't have to wonder if a guy is marrying me for my cooking. He'll be marrying me despite it."

~-~

Lester had spent years taking care of Viola Beckett's money, keeping her scheming father from getting his hands on it, and now she wanted to cut him loose. She wouldn't have had a dime if he hadn't protected her. With his finances the way they were, this was the worst possible time for her to gain some financial independence. If she'd just wait, he'd give her all of it back and then some.

He'd fumed on the drive from the ranch to the airport. But after several hours of looking at figures, he'd come up with a plan.

He could scrape together the two million she wanted. That would shut her up and buy him the time he needed to profit from the rest. He'd email her in the morning and let her know how soon she'd have a check. If he played this right, she'd back off and leave him alone. At least long enough for him to give a reasonable explanation for the losses on her investments.

Two million was a small price to pay for the rest. The interest alone would set him up for life. He was so certain this was the solution to his problems with Viola he couldn't wait until he got to the office. As soon as he reached the airport, he powered up his laptop and began typing.

Dear Viola,

I'd like to apologize for our confrontation. I'm afraid I forgot you were a grown woman with the right to her own money. If you'll let me know where you're banking, I'll have the two million transferred within the week.

After looking at the property you've chosen, I agree it's a good value and has everything you need for your business. I wish you the best of luck with your first home. I think you've picked the right property.

Best wishes,
Lester Charters

As he pushed send he was more sure than ever that he'd found the solution to his Viola Beckett problem.

~-~

Byron had spent the last two days going over the statements from Lester Charters. Not only was he absolutely stunned by the amount of money Vivi had, he was sure something was wrong with the way Charters was handling the fortune.

On the surface the statements spelled out where Charters had her money, but he'd done some searching and most of the funds were ones he was running himself.

If Vivi hadn't claimed Charters was a close personal friend, he'd suspect a Ponzi scheme. He suspected it anyway. He'd put in a call to an old college buddy who was in the banking business and was waiting to hear back. He hadn't said anything to Vivi yet. No use them both being upset, and he was upset.

In his gut, he had the feeling the old man was scamming her. He wondered if it was too late to get any of her money back.

Vivi knocked on the door and without waiting, barged into the room. "I got an email from Mr. Charters. He says he'll wire me the money today if I'll send my banking information. I guess I was wrong about him." Her smile spread across her face, and she danced across the floor to him. "I've been making myself sick thinking Mr. Charters might be a crook."

"What did he say exactly?" Byron stacked the statements into a neat pile and put them on the small desk in the corner.

Pulling her phone out of her pocket, she scrolled then handed it to him. The email sounded right, but again, there was something off. He read it again and again, but couldn't pinpoint what was bothering him.

He forced a smile. "Guess we were wrong. I'm glad."

She walked over to stand before him. "No you're not glad. What's wrong?"

Byron pulled her into a hug then set her back far enough to see her expression. "It's probably nothing. He was so adamant about you not having control of your money. He's reversed direction faster than a spooking colt. Just doesn't make sense."

"What do we do now?"

Byron pulled a shabby note pad from the desk drawer and handed it to Vivi along with a pencil. "I know this might be jumping the gun, but I have a friend in the banking industry. He can explain some things."

"How could a banker know what Mr. Charters is doing?"

"He actually works for the US Securities and Exchange Commission. It's his job to know about investments." What the hell was he getting himself into? He'd worked hard to distance himself from people and drama. Now he was running toward Vivi and her chaos at full speed. He supposed that was what you did for people you loved.

Vivi was asking more questions, but his mind had crashed to a stop at the word love. Did he love her? Stupid question. Of course he did. He'd known for a while, but like a bulled-up colt, he'd refused to admit to the feeling.

His chest felt like that colt had taken aim and given him

its best shot with both hind feet.

"What's wrong?" Vivi stood beside him, her small hand rubbing his arm. He realized he was rubbing the center of his chest. When she left, it was going to be a bitch. Well, he could go with her. Change wasn't always bad, was it?

"Nothing, just thinking."

"Well, stop. You look like you swallowed a lemon."

Yeah, change wasn't always bad. If he repeated that one hundred times, he might even believe it. "I'm going to call my friend right now."

"That's a good starting place. I'll email Mr. Charters with the information necessary for him to wire the money. In the meantime, we'll hope for the best."

That was his Vivi, always looking on the bright side. He'd spent so much of his time on the dark side this woman was like a ray of sunshine on a winter day.

The conversation with his friend didn't net much concrete information, but Michael was going to look into the recent dealing of Charters Ltd.

Byron went to Lester Charters' website, but he couldn't find any information, not that he'd thought he would.

Vivi emailed Charters with her banking information, and she received a quick email back assuring her the process would be started immediately.

"Nothing to do now but wait." Byron closed his laptop and leaned back in the chair.

"Well, I can think of something to do to pass the time." The wicked smile on her face set his blood to racing.

"You haven't ridden Worry for a couple of days," Byron said. "It's cold, but we could bundle up."

"That's a good idea, but I was thinking more along the lines of unbundling."

CHAPTER FOURTEEN

Vivi had put three thousand dollars down as earnest money to hold the Leavenworth property. When the bank received the two million from Mr. Charters, she saw no reason not to pay off the property in full. Daily emails from Mr. Charters assured her he could cash in more mutual funds if she needed extra money for repairs. She'd been worried about him when he'd opposed the purchase, but he'd come through in the end.

She hadn't been this excited since—she'd never been this excited. For the first time in her life, she had a plan and place to call her own. She was moving forward.

Skipping down the stairs like a five-year-old, she nearly collided with Cary.

"You're happy today." Cary gripped Rodie Owen's hand, carefully holding him away from her body. The little boy had mud spatters from head to toe. Cary held his wet, dirty socks in her other hand. "Rodie decided to wash his Tonka Trucks beside the pig pen. The hose ran water into the pens. The pigs decided to join in the fun."

Rodie wiggled, trying to escape his mother's grasp. "Aw, Ma."

Cary looked down at her son, working to retain the

frown on her face. "Upstairs now, young man. You're taking a bath."

"Ma," Rodie said, his voice rising in a whine.

"Is that a whine I hear?" She turned the boy loose and pointed up the stairs. "Put your clothes in the hamper, and I'll meet you in the bathroom." When he hesitated, she said, "Now!"

As Rodie disappeared up the stairs, Cary laughed. "He's all boy. Dirt is his best friend with the pigs next. Now tell me, why the big grin."

"I made an offer on the ranch, and the owners accepted. It's mine." Vivi pulled out her phone and scrolled to some pictures. "It needs some work, but I'm excited about that. I might need your expertise. I haven't ever done anything like this before."

"Neither have I, but Pansy has. I'm sure she'll be able to help. When do we get to see it?"

"I signed the papers yesterday. I own my first home." She fell onto the sofa and stretched her legs out onto the footstool. "I never thought that would happen."

Cary settled into the rocker. "What about Byron?"

Vivi's joy fled faster than a runaway train. She shook her head. "That is the only problem. He wants to stay on the ranch."

"You could stay here. We'd work something out." Cary leaned toward Vivi, concern in her eyes.

"That's just it. He hasn't said one word about me staying." Vivi forced a tight grin. "I can't really invite myself to move in."

Cary nodded. "Have you invited him to go with you?"

"In a roundabout way. He said his home is here on the Circle W." Vivi heaved herself up from the couch, unhappiness weighing her down. "He's been upfront about his plans, and they don't include moving."

"Do you want me to have Micah talk to him?"

A blush heated Vivi's cheeks. That would go over like a skunk at the baptism Friends getting involved in Byron's decisions was not the way to smooth things out between them. "Um, no. Thanks for the offer though. We'll work it out."

Vivi threw on her coat and hurried across the barnyard to Byron's. She pulled the front tight over her body to keep out the cold November air.

When he'd texted her earlier that they needed to talk a tiny spark of hope jumped to life in her brain. For a split second, she wondered if he'd decided they could make a go of it on her new ranch. Then she ruthlessly shut that idea down. No use setting herself up for heartbreak. Byron hadn't once mentioned anything about the future.

After giving a quick knock, she opened the door. Byron sat at the desk, the top filled with papers. She hung the coat on a hook by the door and moved to stand behind him. "Hey, big fella. Looking for a good time?" She ran her fingers through his hair and grinned as he turned to look at her.

"We need to talk."

His tone sounded ominous, and her shoulders tensed. Why couldn't something go smoothly for once? All she really wanted at this point was to have a home and someone to love, but even that seemed out of reach no matter how hard she tried.

She dragged a chair across the floor and pulled it as close to Byron's as she could. Raised gold letters spelling Charters Asset Management Company ran across the tops of most of the heavy, cream colored parchment. Her statements. "What did you find?"

He sorted through the pile and pulled out two statements. He tapped one finger on the top of the pile closest to him. "I sent these to my friend, the one with the SEC. It'll take a few days before we hear anything."

She couldn't wait to share her news. At least in this one area, everything was going as she'd planned. "I think it will be okay. The bank called a little bit ago. Mr. Charters sent two million yesterday so I went ahead and signed on the place."

"Good, good for you." But his expression didn't look like he meant the words.

She'd thought he'd have been as excited as she was by the money, but if this was excitement, she was doing it wrong.

Byron took her hand. "I'm a suspicious bastard. I'd like to have Charters checked out just to be sure."

"Okay, but I'm sure he'll be fine." She wove her fingers through his and watched as he scanned one of the statements again. She was going to miss him when she left.

He ran his finger down a column. "Do you mind my asking how much money you have with him?"

She thought for a moment and found she didn't mind telling Byron anything. Hell, she'd given him the few statements she had in her possession. He was the one person in the world she trusted completely. "I just got an email answering that question. We started with more, but Mr. Charters says the market has been down. There is about eighty-three million right now. He's confident it will come back up in the next couple of years."

The choking sound coming from Byron startled her. Jumping to his feet, he paced around the small room, muttering something she couldn't quite make out. With a piece of paper and a pen from the desk, he sat on the bed, scribbling.

When he finally looked at her again, his face was drawn down into a frown. "Did I hear you right? You have over eighty million dollars?" His face had paled, and he ran his fingers through his hair causing little spikes to stand straight up.

"I actually inherited one hundred and ninety million, give or take a few, when my grandfather died. Well, Sebastian and I did, but it was in a trust until we turned twenty-five. I gave over half of it away, mostly to the Association for the Deaf. Mr. Charters about had a cow, but I felt really strongly about helping others like my brother. The balance has lost some value over the years, according to him."

Byron was pacing across the room, but he froze mid turn when she told him how much money she'd inherited. He stared at her.

She waited for him to laugh, gasp, say something, but he just watched her, his jaws clenched. The silence made her nervous. "I told you I'd inherited some money."

He sank into the desk chair, braced his forearms on his thighs and hung his head. "Nearly two hundred million isn't some money, Vivi. It's all the money."

~-~

No wonder she'd bought a multi-million dollar place without a second thought. "Since you own this place, let's go have another look." The drive to Leavenworth passed some of his favorite spots. Byron had fallen in love with the high desert of central Oregon the first time he'd driven through, and that hadn't lessened in the four years he'd lived here.

"This area is pretty," Vivi said. She'd said the same thing every time they'd driven anywhere, and her word echoed his thoughts. The mountain backdrop against the sage and Juniper trees was a balm for his soul.

"What's the first thing you're going to have fixed on the house?"

She turned from gazing at the scenery and grinned. "I'm going to find a contractor."

Of course she was. Probably several contractors.

"The inside will need painted, and I want to refinish the floors. What kind of wood do you think they are? Not oak."

"They're red fir. Someone must have salvaged them from an old house. You can't buy that anymore."

Her eyes shone. "Really, I like that. I love old things."

"Viv, you do know you're going to have to do more

than paint. The building you're going to use as a studio will need to be gutted. I don't know how much of the plumbing is going to be salvageable.

As they drove, they talked about one project after another until Vivi fell asleep. Byron glanced at her and knew when she was gone, his world wouldn't be as bright.

He turned into the long gravel drive and pulled up to the back of the house. "You know, it wouldn't take much to oil the logs on the outside. That would improve the looks right off. You could make some bent twig rockers. That's what you do, right?"

"I hadn't thought of that, but yes, I could." She climbed the steps and turned a slow circle. "They would be perfect here. And a little table. I could have some western style cushions made. Let's look inside."

She fitted the key into the deadbolt on the front door, grabbed the wrought iron handle and stepped inside. "The first thing this place needs is a good cleaning."

As they wandered through the living room, the view out the picture window caught Byron's attention. Sparkling lights covered the town and tourists crowded the streets. The Washington State Autumn Leaf Festival was in full swing.

"Did you know Leavenworth almost died when the railroad rerouted its tracks in the thirties?

When did they decide to do this and how? Vivi turned to look toward the town, and Byron took the opportunity to watch her, soaking up her beauty for when she was gone. Just once, he wished things had worked out like he wanted. If Viv had stayed in East Hope—. But he'd known that wasn't going to happen from the beginning. She was destined for bigger things. "In a last ditch effort to save their town, the city leaders reshaped a dying logging town into a Bavarian village."

"It's an amazing story. And to think, soon I'll be part of it."

She would be a part of the future of Leavenworth. The

town would receive her intelligence, kindness and warmth.

Good thing he was happy at the Circle W.

He took in the overgrown yard and the collapsed portion of the fence partially hidden in the tall grass. An older Hesston swather and a 90's round baler stood just outside the fence, covered with leaves and dust. They'd been top of the line in their day. He wondered how long it had been since someone had used them.

Vivi had paid too much for this property, that was obvious, but with her money, she could make it a showplace and a home. The thought of her finding a rich bastard to share her life with hurt more than he cared to admit.

"Are you okay? You got really quiet." Vivi stood looking up at him.

"Just thinking of what the house needs before you move in. You'll have to have the plumbing checked and the water tested. And by the looks of the roof, it will have to be replaced, too." They wandered from room to room. Vivi had pulled a notepad from her purse and the list she made got longer by the minute.

"Cary and Micah should be able to recommend a contractor." She scribbled something else on the list then stopped, tapping her pencil against her lip.

"You do realize you're going to need more than one, right?"

Vivi rewarded him with her bright smile. "Sure. We could run into town and pick up some cleaning supplies. I can't wait to start on my new home."

He didn't miss the fact that she'd said 'her new home'. Byron walked her to the front door.

"Why don't you take the truck and get a broom and some cleaning supplies. I'll look around outside."

She caught the keys from mid-air when he tossed them to her. "I'll be back in a few minutes."

After watching Vivi drive away, Byron made his way down the back steps. Weeds and wild Morning Glory covered everything that wasn't moving, but the barn and corrals appeared to be in surprisingly good shape. The realtor had told Vivi that the owner, an elderly rancher, had lived here for most of his adult life. He'd raised hay and cattle on the ranch until he'd had to quit for health reasons. In the years since he'd been moved to a nursing home, the place had stood vacant.

Byron brushed the layer of dust and leaves off the seat of the swather and studied the dials. He'd cut a lot of hay since coming to work for Micah. Micah didn't own this model, but it was known for being a workhorse.

The old girl ground out her displeasure at the first turn of the key then she fired right up. The sound of the engine was smooth as good whiskey, but when he lifted the head, the reel turned like an old man with a broken walker. The creak and groan of the moving parts were like music to his ears.

The Hesston baler was next on his list. Unlike its partner, the machine refused to start. Too bad he wasn't a better mechanic. What he'd like to do more than anything was saddle up one of the colts and ride the land. He walked back toward the house.

His head seemed to be filled with unrealistic desires lately. This wasn't his land, and she wasn't his either.

The hum of the diesel engine announced Vivi's arrival. One last look at the hills and meadow, and he turned back to the house. He'd been worried that Vivi had jumped into this ranch without thinking, which she had. He'd been wrong. With a lot of work, this place would become a good working ranch.

This was the kind of place Byron would like to own if he could move far from the tourists that packed Leavenworth. He'd help her find someone to lease the land. Someone who wouldn't screw her over.

That thought made his skin crawl. No one was going to screw his Vivi. He heard the truck door slam. *Get those thoughts out of your head, Byron.* She wasn't his, and never would be.

Byron met Vivi in the living room and helped her unpack the bags. They spent the next several hours clearing the dust and cobwebs from the rooms, chatting about nothing. Vivi living here with another man popped into his thoughts like an irritating itch, but he banished them with a ruthless sword.

CHAPTER FIFTEEN

Vivi poured her second cup of coffee. Cary, Micah and the kids had gone to East Hope, and the house was unusually quiet. She sat at the kitchen table and enjoyed the sight of the mountains outside the window.

Thank god for her new friends. Discovering the central Oregon area and meeting the people of East Hope was the best thing that had ever happened to her. Pansy and Cary had mad the long drive and helped clean the rest of her new house. They'd camped out in the empty house and had a girl's weekend filled with work, laughter and wine.

Last Saturday, she was amazed to see a long line of cars and trucks come down the driveway. Most of East Hope arrived unannounced to clear the trash and overgrown plants from the yard and barn area.

Clinton and Millie Barnes had stocked her pantry with canned goods from Foodtown and refused to let her pay a dime. Pansy and Kade brought pulled pork and all the fixings to feed the crowd. She'd never known comradery existed to this level and thanked her lucky stars she'd stumbled onto this place. Byron had been disappointingly absent.

Would her new town be as receptive?

She needn't have worried. Various neighbors and business owners had dropped in to welcome her. She'd made the right choice. Only one thing was missing. And that wasn't going to change.

Vivi looked at the yellow pad in front of her and ran her finger down the to-do list. She was staying in East Hope for three more days then she'd move to Leavenworth permanently.

Her art supplies would arrive next week. Several of her new friends had recommended a reputable contractor, and she'd spent hours with him deciding the best way to use the space in the studio. Several walls would have to be moved and another large window installed to give her a big bright showroom. He'd suggested expanding another room to give her more space to work.

Her dream was coming true.

She underlined another contractor's name. A roofer friend of Micah's had recommended a business in the area. His estimate included minor repairs for the house and a metal roof for the studio. The plumber was scheduled to meet with her tomorrow.

As she refilled her cup, Byron entered the back door, his expression somber. She hadn't seen him for several days, and she smiled despite his expression.

"Coffee's fresh. Can I get you a cup."

Byron's shook his head and placed a paper on the table in front of her. "I got an email from my friend."

She glanced at the paper then up at Byron. "What's wrong?"

"My buddy at the Security and Exchange Commission has been checking into your Mr. Charters. Your investor is under investigation."

"For what?" Mr. Charters had handled her trust for years and her grandfather's money before that. "There must be a mistake."

"No mistake. Do you know who Bernie Madoff is?"

Vivi nodded, fear making her muscles stiff. Sharp stings

of anxiety skittered across her skin. "He's that guy that scammed all those people out of their money." Her stomach roiled and her heart skipped a beat. This was going to be bad. Worse than she'd thought.

"Your guy is like Bernie's little brother. Not literally, but still." Byron took her hands in his. "This is off the record, but Charters is under federal investigation for running a Ponzi scheme."

Her head spun as she tried to make sense of what Byron was saying. Mr. Charters had been one of Grandy's best friends. He wouldn't do this to her. He couldn't. "I can't believe this. Somebody's made a mistake."

She pulled out her cell. Her hands were shaking so badly, it took three tries before she had the right number. "I'm calling him. He'll have an explanation." The call to his direct line went straight to voice mail. She hung up and tried the office number with the same results.

Byron's phone pinged. He read the text, and his expression was filled with concern when he met her gaze. "They've arrested Charters."

They walked back to the bungalow. The next several hours were filled with phone calls and waiting. Information came in in bit and pieces none of which told them anything.

Her world had gone from bright to a black hole in the blink of an eye, or a ping of a cell phone. She sat at Byron's desk, her head in her hands the word idiot running in a loop through her brain. "How did I not know this? How could I not have suspected anything?" She dropped her head to the desk with a sigh. She wanted Byron to put his arms around her, to make her feel safe, but he kept his distance. His feelings couldn't have been plainer if he'd shouted them. She was on her own here.

Byron's phone rang, and he put it on speaker. A man's voice came through as if he were in the room. "Byron, I have bad news. This is just preliminary so keep that in mind. But it looks like the money is gone. From what we can see, there are quite a few investors involved. Tell your friend not to count on getting much money back."

"Thanks, Michael. Can you keep us informed?"

The men said their goodbyes, but Vivi wasn't listening. She'd lost interest half way through the conversation. She'd never needed much money, but Byron had been right. She hadn't realized the comfort she'd felt knowing the money was there.

Byron's hands wrapped around her upper arms, and he pulled her to her feet. He didn't wrap his arms around her, but his voice was soft. "There was no reason not to trust the man. He'd managed your money for years with no problem."

She wanted to believe him, but she knew this was her fault.

"Michael recommended a lawyer, and I already sent him an email." He put a finger under her chin and tilted her head up. "It will work out."

Vivi didn't believe him, and she couldn't be strong any more. The tears flowed until she was gasping for breath. "What am I going to do?"

"You've got two million dollars. That's more than most people. We'll figure it out."

"I used all of that to pay for the property. I have no money to fix it up or to even pay the taxes." She looked at him, her eyes red, her breathing hitched. "I have a few thousand dollars in the bank, but I'll need that to live on until I find a job. I'll have to sell before I can even move in."

~-~

Even with tear-reddened eyes, Vivi was the most amazing woman Byron had ever met, and Byron was having a hard time keeping his self-induced detachment.

He pulled a handkerchief from his pocket and wiped her face. "My granddaddy always said, 'Don't cry over spilt milk'. If you're going to have to sell, let's make a plan."

"All I have to plan for is how to sell the property and get some of my money back."

Byron took her hand and pulled her out the door to his pickup. "We might as well go look at it."

"You want to drive all the way to Leavenworth to look at the property I can't afford to keep?"

"Have you got anything better to do?" He pulled onto the highway and sped down the road. "Tell me what you'd planned for the place when money was no object."

She turned, her expressive eyes filled with sadness. "Money is a big object now."

"Work with me here. What did you have planned?" He kept one hand on the wheel and with the other reached over to smooth her hair. "First thing."

She pulled a tissue from her purse and wiped her eyes. "I'm supposed to meet with the plumber in the morning. I've already talked to a contractor about remodeling the shop by the road. I'll have to cancel them both."

Vivi was silent for a moment then she jerked her gaze to Byron's. "John Walker, the rancher on the next place, called me yesterday about renting the property. I'll have to call him back."

The rest of the drive, Byron racked his brain for more comforting words, any comforting words, but came up with nothing. It was a relief to pull into the driveway.

As they rounded the front of the truck, Byron touched Vivi's shoulder. "Let's take this one step at a time. Maybe Charters has all the money in a bank account somewhere, and you'll get it back. Miracles do happen." His attempt at positivity was weak, but he was grasping at straws here.

"Not to me they don't." The tears had stopped for the moment, but he could see her struggle. "I'm going to have to sell."

He pulled her toward the house and when they reached the porch he held out his hand. "Key?"

She dug through her purse and handed it to him. When

they were inside he heard her choke back more tears, but when he turned, she'd wiped them away. She stood in the center of the room, her hands at her sides, a desolate look on her face.

"We might be able to figure out something. Maybe you won't have to sell." A niggling idea kept working its way into his head. "Since you paid cash for the property, you don't have a loan payment."

"I could get a job in town, but what about the property taxes? And the upkeep? I can't do all the repairs by myself." She walked over to the picture window and propped her butt on the sill. "I have to accept the facts. It's my fault I'm in this situation. I didn't take care of business."

"This isn't all your fault. The man is a crook. He screwed lots of people." The thought of the dapper Mr. Charters cheating Vivi out of her money made Byron want to grab him by his scrawny neck and squeeze.

She looked around the room. "I love this place. I'll be sorry to see it go." Standing, she dusted her hands against the legs of her jeans.

Two enormous Cottonwoods on either corner of the yard were flanked by smaller pines. The trees framed a view of the closest hay field and a large pond. What a way to start each day. Sitting here with a cup of coffee, looking out at your land.

At the edge of the yard, sat the machinery. Even though they needed a little work, there was no reason to give it to the new owners. Vivi could get a bit of her money back by selling them separately.

The ride through the property and a conversation with a neighbor had confirmed his suspicions. The old man who'd owned the place had been a good cowboy. He'd raised meadow hay on the irrigated fields that came with the ranch and grazed cattle on the timbered hillsides. This was a working ranch, and it wouldn't take much work to run cattle here in the spring. The place was big enough to make a living. A man wouldn't get rich, but he could have a good life.

All Vivi needed was cattle—and experience—and money. He couldn't forget the money. For the first time in his life, he wished he were rich, or even on speaking terms with his father.

He could imagine what dear old dad would say if he called wanting to borrow money. Even more horrifying to his father would be borrowing money for a ranch. The lecture would begin immediately and last until the moon outshone the sun. And he still wouldn't loan a dime to Byron. Help from his family was out of the question.

He had about thirty head of mama cows he'd managed to buy during his years at the Circle W. One of the perks of working for Micah was being allowed to run some of his own cows. Too bad thirty head wasn't enough to make a living.

His gaze wandered to the machinery again. Vivi could sell the hay.

"I promised myself when Father died that I'd find a way to do what I love and be happy. I should have known this was too easy. Let's go back to the ranch and call a realtor."

As she turned toward the door he caught her hand and pulled her into his arms. "I didn't know you were a quitter."

She stiffened and tried to push away but he held her tight. "You might have to sell in the end, but at least we can try to find a way to make this work." A branch scratched against the side of the house, and the wind whistled through the chimney as the sky darkened. The predicted storm had arrived.

Vivi leaned back and stared up at him. "Look, I appreciate all you've done to help me. I really do, but I can't see a way out of this. I'm not quitting. I'm being practical."

"Practicality is overrated. We need imagination and

inspiration, creativity with a touch of whimsy. We need a daydreamer, and you do that as well as anyone I've ever met." He stroked his finger across her forehead, brushing back a strand of hair.

"Daydreaming has gotten me exactly nothing."

"There you go giving up again. I don't know about you, but I'm not going down without a fight." He backed her against the wall, placing a hand on either side of her head then brushed his lips against hers. "We can make this work."

"We?" A tremor wobbled through the single word. Her eyes were wide as she stared into his.

"I know. I'm as surprised as you are." And he was. All this time he'd been guarding his heart, keeping himself apart, when all he needed was this brave, kind, happy woman. "I think I love you."

This time the corners of her mouth quivered. "You think?"

"Once in a while I do." He touched a fingertip to the corner of her mouth, and the grin got wider. "This is new to me so cut me some slack."

She tilted her head and threaded her fingers through his. Her smile widened.

"For a woman who talks all the time, you sure aren't saying much."

"Well, if it makes it any easier on you, I love you too. I have since the first time you gave me a riding lesson, and I watched you with that stubborn colt. I knew you were the man for me." She threw her arms around his neck. "I still don't see how we can keep this place."

"We probably can't, but we can give it a try." Damn, he should have thought this through. The first time in years that he did something spontaneous—.

"Look, we can sell this property and move back to East Hope. I like it there."

She'd given him a way out. She was willing to give up everything she'd worked for to make him happy.

Her excitement had dropped away, and her expression was serious. "We'll figure out something."

For a moment there, he'd dared to hope. There was no way he could make her happy. No matter what she said, she'd been raised with money. She had no idea how hard it was to make it in ranching without a big checkbook or family. The struggle would wear her down and the light in her eyes that he loved would fade.

He changed the subject. "On second thought, I think you should move in here like you'd planned. Even if you have to sell, it will be more appealing to buyers if someone lives here."

CHAPTER SIXTEEN

Wow! One moment they'd seemed to be a team, working to figure out a problem, the next, he was moving her out on her own and crawling back into his hole at the Circle W.

Vivi carried the foam pad into the house along with her one set of sheets. A full bed lay in pieces in the back of the truck she'd borrowed from Micah along with a small dresser from the Salvation Army.

Cary had found a dining table and two chairs in to top of the barn, and Micah had delivered them. If Vivi hadn't been so confused, she'd have been delighted with the circa 1950's chrome and red Formica set. With cast offs from Cary and Pansy, she had enough kitchen utensils to get by. She wouldn't be here very long anyway.

Byron was right about one thing. The property would sell faster if she was here.

She busied herself setting the kitchen to order. And when the few pieces of silverware, dishes and pots and pans were in their place, she stood back and took in the room. From the log walls to the beams on the ceiling, this was the home of her dreams.

Her father had been right all along. He'd tried to warn

her. She'd been born with a brain wired for one thing, he'd said. When God gave you a natural ability to decipher physics, it was a crime to do otherwise.

She'd been searching for personal and professional happiness and someone to love her. Looks like she's have to settle for professional happiness alone.

Trying to be positive in these circumstances was exhausting, but the alternative was unthinkable. Sebastian's life had been cut short before he even got to live. She wasn't wasting hers. She'd enjoy the house for as long as she had it, be it days or months. And she'd hold tight to her memories of her time with Byron.

For a few days, she'd held her breath every time her phone rang. Each time it wasn't him, she'd been disappointed. He'd declared his love for her then let fear and doubt stop him from finding happiness. She couldn't live like that anymore.

She backed the pickup up to the porch then wedged out the headboard and carried it into the house. Without too many mistakes, she had the frame put together. The bed frame looked lost in the big master bedroom.

Reaching into the truck bed, she tried to pull the mattress out, but she couldn't get any leverage. She climbed in and braced her back against the front of the bed and pushed with her feet. The mattress and box springs inched toward the open tailgate. One more push and they tilted out until one edge rested on the porch.

She stood back and looked. They'd be filthy if she dragged them across the porch, but if she were going to sleep here tonight, she'd have to figure out how to get them to the bedroom.

The sound of tires crunching on gravel caught her attention. Byron's truck pulled up beside hers, a recliner in the back. "Need some help?" He jumped to the ground, not making eye contact.

No way was she getting her hopes up again. He was a nice guy, and one day when she stopped loving him, he'd be a good friend, but just now, with her life falling apart, she didn't need him reminding her of all she'd lost.

She wondered if in some obscure language, her middle name translated to stubborn. "No, I have it thanks." She turned back to the mattress and lifted it until it stood on edge. Maybe if she balanced it on her back...

As she bent to lift, the weight was suddenly gone. Byron had picked it up as if it weighed nothing. After years of grain sacks and hay bales, that's what it probably felt like to him.

"Hey, I had that." Indignation was way better than hopelessness, and she was learning to do outrage well. "I'm not weak."

He just smiled. "Open the screen door, please."

What would have taken her an hour, took him just minutes. He turned to her, fighting a grin. "I'll need some help with the box springs." As he walked from the room, couldn't keep her gaze from dropping to the sight of his butt in the tight Wranglers.

He turned in the doorway and caught her gawking. "See anything you like?"

Hot red embarrassment covered her cheeks and neck. She was not going to play his game. She couldn't even figure out what his game was, and she was tired. "No," she said, suddenly so weary she wasn't sure she could stay on her feet.

Byron came back to her. "Hey, I was kidding."

"Really, because I'm not sure if you know what you're doing." She walked past him to the kitchen, grabbed a Coke from the refrigerator and sank onto one of the kitchen chairs. "I only know I don't want to play anymore. I'm having enough trouble keeping myself going. I can't do that for you, too."

Byron stared at her for a moment then walked out the front door. He managed to get the box springs to the bedroom by himself and set up the bed. By the time she'd finished the soda, he had the bed made and was back out at his truck.

The aroma of pizza hit her like a runaway truck. She had skipped breakfast and hadn't thought of lunch. Her phone said it was four o'clock.

Byron popped the top off a beer and handed it to her. He placed a couple of pieces of pizza on a paper towel in front of her then helped himself.

She inhaled both slices and reached for another. Byron ate silently, but didn't take his eyes off her.

"What!" She'd tried to remain indifferent, but she couldn't stand the scrutiny another minute. "What do you want from me? You act like we're getting closer then you pull away. If you want to be friends, I'm afraid you're in for a big disappointment. I can't be your friend right now. It hurts too much."

He stood and started toward her. When he reached her side, he knelt down. "Vivi, you're so special, but I can't give you want you want, what you deserve."

"Why? I don't understand. You love me. You said so. And I love you so much it hurts. Where's the problem?"

"I'm a loner and I like it like that." Byron stood. "I wish I could say something to make it easier, but I think we should make a clean break." He turned and walked to his truck.

She heard the deep rumble of his Dodge fade into the distance as she sat absorbing his words. "It'd be easier to make a clean break if you'd stay away."

As she worked getting settled into her new, temporary home, she searched for the positive attitude she'd worked so hard to perfect. The only positive thing she could come up with wasn't much, but lately it seemed as if small positives were all she got. At least she hadn't had to carry the mattress and box springs into the house by herself.

Fatigue dragged her down like a heavy weight. As she entered the bedroom, she stopped. Byron had made up the bed. The bright handmade quilt that had lain folded on the end of his was spread out over hers.

~-~

Byron cinched up the gray and white paint colt and swung into the saddle. The animal was coming along nicely, and he'd considered keeping him for his own. The temperature hovered just above freezing, and he tied his wild rag a little tighter around his neck.

The stock in the pens near the barn, were fed and the chores done, but he couldn't force himself to go back into the bungalow and be alone with his thoughts. Going to the big house and watching Micah and Cary shoot him pitying looks wasn't his idea of fun either.

He missed Vivi. He'd gone Leavenworth to give her his grandmother's quilt as a housewarming gift. Why he'd thought he could say good-bye and be done when he hadn't been able to do it before baffled him.

In the two weeks since he'd walked out of her house, he hadn't heard a word from her or about her. Either she wasn't communicating with Cary and Micah, or they weren't telling him if she did.

And to top things off, his father had called for the first time in four years. The man had the nerve to tell him to come home. Dear old dad had disowned Byron over football and now he needed help. He didn't apologize or ask. He demanded, threatening, always threatening.

If Vivi had been here, she'd have made him look at the whole picture, calmed him, kissed him until he couldn't think.

He missed her laugh. He just plain missed her. How stupid was he? He'd had the perfect woman, she'd loved him and he'd thrown that away.

When he'd chosen ranching over football, his dad had called him selfish. The man had called Byron a loser. Maybe he was both. Maybe it was time to change.

He sat in the silence of the timber on the hill above the ranch. The colt cocked a hip and dropped his head. The wind rustled the pine boughs, and he heard a turkey call in the distance.

He'd thought he loved this ranch above anything, but it was just a place. He loved Vivi. He'd valued his solitude to the exclusion of people, but he didn't want to be alone anymore.

He turned the horse toward the barn. He had his work cut out for him if he wanted her to forgive him and learn to trust him again. As he unsaddled, he thought back to their last conversation. How tired and downtrodden she'd looked. She'd told him she didn't want just friendship, but did she still want more? All his life, he'd been single minded when it had come to something he wanted.

Now, finally, he'd decided he wanted Vivi.

Cary waved from the porch, calling his name. He waved back and drove away. He didn't want to chat, he didn't want to waste time, and he didn't need any advice. It was up to him to make things right with Vivi or live with the consequences.

He'd driven by Unique Log Furnishings in Yakima, Washington but had never been inside. It more than met his expectations. By the time he was done, he'd cleaned out a big chunk of his checking account and filled the bed of his pickup. It took some fast-talking to get the owner to sell him a floor model. There'd been a time when nothing could have gotten him to beg, but he was on a mission and nothing, not even his hermit tendencies, would stop him.

With a bottle of what the clerk at the grocery store assured him was their best wine, and a plastic tray of cheese and crackers, he started for Vivi's. He wasn't a wine drinker, but if she turned him down, he could drown his sorrows.

He could see the old truck Micah had loaned Vivi in front of the house. It hadn't occurred to him she might not be home until he was almost there. He hadn't been this nervous staring down a three hundred pound defensive lineman. Vivi weighed a little over one hundred pounds, but she could destroy him without lifting a finger.

He turned off the key and silence surrounded him. All he had to do was get out of the truck and—. He heard the wooden screen door slam and looked up to see the love of his life standing at the top of the steps, arms crossed beneath her breasts. He raised his gaze to the scowl on her beautiful face.

"I told you I don't want to be friends. Go away."

He climbed down, the bag with the wine and food in his hand. "I brought you dinner. Well not exactly dinner, but snacks. I brought snacks and wine." God he sounded like a high school girl, whiny and wordy.

"I've had dinner. Go away." He'd known she'd be standoffish at first, but she was normally a kind woman. This wasn't going at all like he'd planned. Squinted eyes and thinned lips were a dead giveaway that she wasn't overjoyed to see him. That, and the fact that she kept telling him to go away.

"Vivi, give me a couple of minutes. Then if you want, I'll leave." He held out the sack as a sort of peace offering.

She turned on her heel and went into the house. By the time he caught up with her, she sat in the recliner, the only piece of furniture in the house. Her arms were still crossed, so instead of starting the conversation, he went into the kitchen and poured them both a glass of wine.

She took hers and didn't immediately throw it at him.

He took that as a good sign. "I know I've been…" He had to be careful, choose the perfect words.

"A fool, an idiot, a closed off, unreachable loner?" She didn't smile and her harsh words chilled him to the core.

"All of those and hard to read, a coward and unfair."

"And you think telling me this will what? Make me want you around?" She took a sip of the wine, grimaced and put the glass on the floor. "We've been through this before. I want more."

Byron knelt in front of her, taking her hands in his. "Viola Margaret Beckett, I know you have no reason to trust me, but I love you."

"Yeah, you said that before. It didn't keep you from pushing me away when I got too close." She gently tugged her fingers from his and clenched her hands in her lap. She was as closed off as he'd ever been. "My father was right. I'm going to sell this place and go back home. I have my degree. I can teach. I was a fool to think I could change things."

He remained where he was, even when she leaned away. "We can change things. Look, I've been thinking. We can make a go of this place."

"Until you decide to leave again."

He took her cheeks in his hands and looked into her eyes. "I'm not leaving. You're the best thing that ever happened to me and for a long time I was too stupid—no, too scared to admit it." He stroked a fingertip along her jaw line, marveling at her soft smooth skin. He raised his gaze to hers and continued. "I'll do stupid things in the future. If I run true to course, I'll do lots of them. But I'll never leave you again."

"I don't believe you." Her expression had softened, but her body remained stiff.

He kissed her again, twice. "Trust me. Have you ever known me to lie?"

"No, you've never lied." She watched him, her gaze roaming over his face. "You said we could make it on this place. Does that mean you and me—here—together? Forever?"

The last word came out as a whisper, and he had another jolt of guilt with the knowledge of how much he'd hurt her. "I have around thirty head of mama cows. That's not enough to make a living on, but we have good hay fields here. We can sell what we don't use until we build up our herd. I can get a job on one of the ranches." He glanced at his boots. "You'd have to get a job in town until we get on our feet."

At the touch of her finger on his cheek, he looked up.

"I don't mind working. Several of the art galleries in Sisters have help wanted signs."

He pulled her to her feet and into his arms. His fear of leaving the Circle W was gone. It had disappeared like a puff of smoke the moment he realized Vivi was the most important thing in his life.

She put a hand on his chest and pushed him back a few inches. "You said forever. Does that mean marriage?"

He reached into his pocket and fished out a plain, battered silver band. "This was my grandmother's. This was all they could afford when they first got married. They were married for fifty-nine years. I can get you a fancier one when we get ahead."

She held out her, hand and he slipped the ring on her finger. "I like this one. It's got a record of longevity. I like the sound of nearly sixty years of marriage."

He kissed her hard and clung to her. "Are you saying yes?" He couldn't quite believe she'd forgiven him, that she was his.

"Yes, yes, yes, forever yes."

When he'd finished kissing any lingering doubt right out of her, he took her hand and led her out to the pickup.

"It's beautiful, but why a bed? We could use some furniture for the living room." She ran her hand over the big knot in the center of the headboard.

"You didn't think we could both sleep in that little bed you've got in there, did you?"

"You must have been pretty certain I'd forgive you to spend this much." She crawled over the side of the truck, sat on the edge of the bed and wrapped her arms around his neck.

"I wasn't sure at all, but I decided if I was all in on this with you, it was time to start taking chances.

STEPHANIE BERGET

EPILOGUE

Byron sat in a plastic lawn chair on the porch of their new home and watched Vivi work the crowd. Vivi was as out-going as he was introverted. They made a pretty good combination.

Cary and Micah had offered the ranch as a site for their wedding, and he'd tried to look excited. Vivi watched his reaction then told Cary her dream wedding had always been an elopement.

He'd had been worried Vivi would be disappointed at getting married in a courthouse, but once again, he'd underestimated his woman. She'd made arrangements with the Winnemucca Floral and Wedding Chapel. By the time the service was done, she'd become friends with the owners.

He'd never seen her more radiant in the pale pink lace dress. Watching Vivi's eyes fill with tears when the Justice of the Peace pronounced them man and wife was second only to kissing his bride.

Since he hadn't given Vivi the fancy wedding she deserved, he'd made an attempt to visit with all the guests at the reception Cary planned for them. The only small talk he was good at was cattle and ranching, though, and he was at a total loss with some of the people.

His wife knew him well. When she'd seen his discomfort, she'd taken his hand and placed him on the end of the porch, away from everyone. People wandered across the lawn and in and out of the house, but only Micah approached him.

"Congratulations." Micah gave him a slap on the back. "Vivi will have you in shape in no time."

"I don't know if I'll ever be comfortable in a crowd, but it's better when I know she's here with me."

As they talked, Vivi made eye contact with him across the yard then sauntered toward him, oblivious to the others. He stood as she approached and when she reached him, she wrapped her arms around his waist. Lifting onto her tiptoes, she kissed him. "Having fun?"

He kissed her back then looked out over their friends and family. There was a time, not so long ago, that he'd thought he was happy alone. Not anymore. He smiled down at the woman who'd rescued him from himself. "I'm not sure I'd call this exactly fun, but as long as you stick with me, Viola Margaret, I can do anything."

Romance Beneath A Rodeo Moon
If you enjoyed reading Sweet Cowboy Kisses, you can find Cary and Micah's story in _Gimme Some Sugar_, the first in the Sugar Coated Cowboys series.

Gimme Some Sugar-Pastry chef, Cary Crockett, is on the run. Pursued by a loan shark bent on retrieving gambling debts owed him by her deadbeat ex-boyfriend, she finds the perfect hiding place at the remote Circle W Ranch. More at home with city life, cupcakes and croissants than beef, beans and bacon, she has to convince ranch owner Micah West she's up to the job of feeding his hired hands. The overwhelming attraction she feels toward him was nowhere in the job description.

Micah West has a big problem. The camp-cook on his central Oregon ranch has up and quit without notice, and his crew of hungry cowboys is about to mutiny. He agrees to hire Cary on a temporary basis, just until he finds the right man to fill the job. Maintaining a hands-off policy toward his sexy new cook becomes tougher than managing a herd of disgruntled wranglers. http://amzn.to/1UDCemK

More books by Stephanie Berget featuring rodeo cowboys, ranchers and the women who love them:

Radio Rose-Cowboys and aliens … on a dark, deserted highway, it can be hard to tell the difference.

Especially when Rose Wajnowski makes her living as a night DJ chatting about alien encounters with folks in tinfoil helmets. Her listeners are eccentric, to say the least. But she's happy—sort of—with her solitary life. Until a midnight car crash and a blow to the head has her seeing tall, handsome extra-terrestrials instead of stars.

Adam Cameron, raised by his narcissistic grandfather, got out of Tullyville, Colorado the day he turned eighteen. He's back ten years later for the reading of his grandfather's will, but he's not happy to be home. Except for meeting the pretty little brunette who nearly ran him down with her car on that dark highway.

Adam is about to be pulled into a contest for a vast fortune and the future of a town he'd just as soon forget. But the quirky inhabitants of Tullyville desperately need his help if their town is to survive. Luckily for him, this cowboy has feisty Rose at his side, and in his arms.

As they work together to save their town, Rose and Adam learn important lessons about trust and the real meaning of family.
http://amzn.to/267wmd6

Sugarwater Ranch-Sean O'Connell's life is perfect, or it was until his partying lifestyle affected his bull riding. Now he's ended the season too broke to leave the Northwest for the warm southern rodeos. When a wild night with his buddies gets out of hand, he wakes up naked, staring into the angry eyes of a strange woman. His infallible O'Connell charm gets him nowhere with the dark-haired beauty. It's obvious she's not his usual good-time girl, so why can't he forget her?

Bar-manager Catherine Silvera finds a waterlogged, unconscious cowboy freezing to death in front of the Sugarwater Bar. She saves his life--then runs faster than a jackrabbit with a coyote on its tail. Any man who makes his living rodeoing is bad news, especially if he thinks partying is part of the competition. He's everything she doesn't want in a man, so why can't she shake her attraction to the rugged cowboy?
http://amzn.to/29lydml

Changing A Cowboy's Tune: Rodeo Road series, book 1.
When her fiancé demands Mavis abandon her goal of barrel racing at the National Finals Rodeo, she chooses to follow her dream and loses the man she adores.

Dex wants nothing more than to marry the woman he loves and build a future on his family's ranch, but when he pushes her to settle into life as a mother and rancher's wife, she bolts. Years apart haven't dampened their desire, but can they see past their own dreams for the future and invent a life they both love?

https://www.amazon.com/Changing-Cowboys-Tune-Rodeo-

Road/dp/1546814892/ref=asap_bc?ie=UTF8

Gimme Some Sugar Excerpt

Snapping his head up, he whirled around, almost elbowing the woman standing behind him. Pulling in a deep, slow breath, partly to gather some semblance of calm and partly to adjust to the tingle where her hand met his arm, he took a step back before speaking.

"Help me with what?" Did he know her? He was sure he didn't, but man….

"I'm sorry. I didn't mean to eavesdrop, but I heard you say you're looking for a cook." Golden eyes the color of whiskey stared into his. "I cook."

He let his gaze wander over her, liking what he saw. She wasn't a local. Her white blond hair was as short as a man's on the sides and curled longer on the top and back. He hadn't seen any woman, or anyone at all who wore their hair like this. Of course, tastes of the people of East Hope ran to the conservative.

Despite the severe hairstyle, she was pretty. Beyond pretty. Leather pants showed off her soft curves, miniature combat boots encased her small feet and a tight tank top enhanced her breasts.

When she cleared her throat, he jerked his eyes up to her face. "It won't do you any good to talk to my breasts. Like most women, it's my brain that answers questions."

A smart ass and she'd caught him red-handed. His cheeks warmed. Damn it, he was blushing. This woman was not at all what he needed. Time to end this. "I have a ranch, the Circle W. We need a camp cook. A man."

Her eyes narrowed, and her body tensed. "It looks like you need any kind of cook you can get." She held her hand out, indicating the empty café. "Not a lot of takers."

She had him there. His gut told him he was going to regret this, but she was right. He had no choice. "I'll hire you week to week." When she nodded, he continued. "I've got seven ranch hands. You'll cook breakfast and dinner and pack lunches, Monday through Friday and serve

Sunday dinner to the hands who are back by six o'clock."

She bounced on the toes of her feet until she noticed him watching her then she pulled on a cloak of calm indifference. "You won't regret this."

He felt a smile touch the corners of his mouth as his gut twisted. "I already do."

http://amzn.to/1UDCemK

ABOUT THE AUTHOR

Stephanie Berget was born loving horses and found her way to rodeo when she married her own, hot cowboy. She and her husband traveled throughout the Northwest while she ran barrels and her cowboy rode bucking horses. She started writing to put a realistic view of rodeo and ranching into western romance. Stephanie and her husband live on a farm, located along the Oregon/Idaho border. They raise hay, horses and cattle, with the help of Dizzy Dottie, the Border Collie and Cisco, team roping horse extraordinaire.

Stephanie is delighted to hear from readers. Reach her at
http://www.stephanieberget.com
Facebook:
https://www.facebook.com/stephaniebergetwrites/
Twitter: https://twitter.com/StephanieBerget